A Court Where I'm Freezing My A** Off

A Made from Magic Novella

Marianne A Scott

To my amazing wonderfully supportive parents. Thank you for always believing in me.

.

.

.

You can go ahead and skip Chapter Three.

CONTENT WARNINGS

Hello reader!

This novella is meant to be read between *Made to Conquer* and *Made to Rule*. It contains spoilers for the first two books in the Made from Magic Series. However, it does not need to be read to understand the plot of *Made to Rule*, so if any of the following themes are triggering, please take care of your mental health.

Sexually explicit scenes that include kink exploration (mainly erotic asphyxiation)

Rejected Mates

Anxiety

Depression

Please note there is no happy ending in this novella since Edina's story is just getting started.

Chapter One

Edina

"FUCK ME, IT'S COLD."

Just minutes ago, I was in a warm study in Northern Italy with my best friend, a werewolf, and a vampire. Now I'm in a drafty, worn-down cabin in the middle of a frozen tundra. Total downgrade if you ask me.

The cabin is made completely of white wood, from the scratched floorboards to the thin walls that don't quite keep out the winter wind. It's completely bare save for the portal entrance, which is still swirling with blue and purple mist from our arrival.

We exit the cabin, and the door almost flies off the hinges from the hurricane-like winds. Plush snow rushes into my boots and I release a frustrated huff that crystalizes in the air. I haven't been cold since I emerged but something about the snow in my shoes makes me miserable. And we just got here.

"What part of *Winter Court* did you not understand, Edina?" Vlad deadpans as he follows me through the door, slamming it shut behind him and shifting the bag he's carrying for me to his other hand. He adjusts his black traveling cloak and dramatically sweeps it behind him, only for the wind to tangle it around his legs again. He hisses, baring his fangs at the swirling gusts, looking ever the part of a stereotypical vampire. In the mortal realm, he can almost pass for a businessman who has a penchant for three-piece suits, but in Faerie, he can flaunt his natural vampiric tendencies.

"Want to give me some cover, Tinker Bell?" he asks as the snow pelts down, dampening his short blonde hair and pale skin.

I sneer. Instead of using my magic to protect him, I harness the moisture in the air to form a little bubble over my head, making my own little icy umbrella. I fluff my blonde hair dramatically and shake off the snow that's collected on my wings.

The vampire gives me a toothy smile. "You're acting like a Fae already." My ego deflates. I've only met one Fae before, and he was fine, but everything I've learned about the rest suggests they're not kind or gentle creatures. Especially the Fae from the Winter Court.

I acquiesce and throw up a shield around Vlad, manipulating the snow so it doesn't touch his skin. He nods his thanks.

"I expected..." All around us, for miles, is nothingness. It's what I imagine the North Pole to look like, all ice and snow and darkness. "More."

I don't know why the barren landscape is getting to me. Maybe it's because I spend most of my time seeking out the sun. I spent every school break I could on my parents' private island in the Maldives. I'd live in a bikini if I could.

Or maybe it's because there's a very real chance I'll need to move here.

A tear slips down my cheek, turning to ice as it plunks into the soft snow. I swear I've cried more this week than I have in my entire life. I was perfectly happy being a semi-powerful witch with Water Magic. But then I emerged as Fae, which was fucking painful, by the way. It's not like it is in movies where a girl wakes up and suddenly has pretty wings and heightened magic. *No.* Wings have to break through bone and muscle and skin all while your ears stretch into points like the most painful piercing ever.

Once I realized what was happening, I knew I'd be hunted and killed in my realm. It's why my best friend took me into hiding and roped herself into working with the Dark Witches to restore the balance of the Kingdom of Magic. She was trying to save me from going to Faerie, but I had to come anyway to secure allies for their war.

For a second, I was even excited about coming to Faerie.

And then Vlad told me I was the missing Princess of the Winter Court, and it didn't take me long to figure that staying in Faerie would be required. They're not going to let a princess return to the mortal realm, especially since, according to Vlad, I'm the queen's only child.

Katie doesn't know yet. She has so much on her plate, I don't want to add to it until I know for certain.

Okay, I chickened out. *Hard.* But the reasoning behind it is sound. So I'm a morally responsible chicken.

"You need to get it together, princess," Vlad snaps, his blue eyes piercing even in the darkness.

"Right." I swipe away another frozen tear and square my shoulders. "Where to?"

He nods forward, and we continue our trek through the snow. We walk in silence, my mind swirling like the snow around us as I try not to add the existing storm. Whenever I get overwhelmed, my powers are uncontrolled. Last time I almost impaled Katie on an icicle.

"The portal is in the Wastelands for a reason," Vlad offers. "It's meant to scare people off. The actual court isn't too bad."

"Really?" I ask, hope sparking in my chest for the first time in days.

"No," he sighs. "It's all snow and ice. But it's the beautiful kind of snow and ice."

I grunt as I tuck a strand of hair behind my pointed ears. "And the queen? Is she as bad as I think she's going to be?"

"Your mother—"

"My mother is the witch who raised me," I snap, and Vlad tugs my elbow until I meet his intense stare.

"It is not your mother's fault you were stolen," he says sternly. "You'd do best to remember that when you meet her. Mention of your human family is a really good way to make sure they end up dead."

"Holy shit," I breathe. "She's that bad?"

"She's Fae." Vlad shrugs like that's an excuse. "And she's held a position of power for millennia, so she's ruthless."

My throat works. My parents—my adoptive parents—aren't parents of the year by any stretch of the imagination. I guess they were involved in the first few years of my life, but as soon as I was old enough, I was shipped to a magical boarding school. I spent holidays with them on the island or in their penthouse in Manhattan, but we gave each other space. At this moment, I've never been more grateful for the people who raised me, even if they were absent. Who knows what I would have ended up like under the care of the Winter Court Queen?

"But you shouldn't hold that against her," Vlad continues. "You're the daughter who was stolen from her. Just because she wouldn't react kindly to people complicit in your capture doesn't mean she won't love you above all else."

"You think my parents knew about this?" I ask, my stomach sinking. There's no way my parents knew I was Fae. They would have warned me.

Vlad sighs. "Give the queen a chance. And, for now, pick up your big girl panties and get your shit together. Every court would love to get their hands on you, so we need to get to the palace before we're ambushed."

"You could just run us there."

"You could just fly us there."

"I don't know how to do that yet," I whisper. My wings flutter behind me like they're trying to prove me wrong. "I tried this morning, but..."

It was a mess, honestly. Thankfully I landed on a mattress and not on the rock floors of the Highland Coven, but I had no control. When I tried to slow down, I sped up. So, I tried to speed up, and then I wound up corkscrewing until I was nauseous.

"Then we're at an impasse," Vlad says, and we continue trudging through the soft powder. I take a deep breath of the cold air, and somehow it invigorates me. The cold is singing to my power, urging me to try things I'd never dream of doing, like teleportation.

Damn, that's annoying. It's really hard to hate the cold when it makes you feel more powerful.

Vlad and I keep walking in silence. Without anything to distract me but the sound of our footsteps, my mind races. I have a million questions, but one keeps needling me, demanding to be asked. "Have you met a Fae named Puck?"

"Yes."

"He's in Spring Court."

"Yes."

"I met him in the mortal realm before I emerged." We met in a dive bar around the corner from my school. We drank, a lot, and when he asked if I'd go home with him, I agreed. It was nothing out of the ordinary until he brought me to the portal in Salem and asked me to realm jump. I said yes, and followed him to the Spring Court, with its forests and flowers and warmth.

It was just something temporary that I could write off as a stupid decision I made when I was younger. One night of crazy hot sex and then back to my life in the mortal realm.

But it's been days and I keep thinking about him. Which is unheard of in my world. I'm a one-and-done kind of girl, and very happy to stay that way.

"He asked me to stay," I admit. "He told me I'd emerge soon, and that I should do it in Faerie."

Vlad lets the silence stretch. "Was there a question attached to that revelation?"

I glare my most withering glare. "Did...do you think he knew? Who I was?"

Vlad considers, his head cocking to the side as he thinks. "Probably," he says after another pregnant pause. "Your kidnapping is common knowledge, and you look exactly like your mother." My heart sinks into my stomach, the nervous butterfly feeling turning to angry hornets.

"Puck works for his queen," Vlad continues. "I wouldn't be surprised if she sent him to the mortal realm to search for you to use against Winter Court. Spring and Winter have been at odds for centuries."

"And if I emerged in Spring Court, they would have killed me?"

"Not at first," Vlad offers. "But it wouldn't have been garden parties and great sex."

I swallow, my hands balling into fists and the snow around us thickening. This is why I don't get attached to people. Everyone has a motive. Everyone will hurt you if you give them the chance.

Vlad watches me but doesn't ask any other questions as I try to get control of my powers. When the snow settles back into its usual pounding and my magic no longer affects it, he says, "So you knew you'd emerge.

"I didn't believe him. I didn't want to believe–"

"Shh." The crunch of ice nearby has my ears twitching, and Vlad grabs my arm, bringing me to a stop. I manifest a ball of ice in my hand as his fangs lengthen, preparing for an ambush.

Fae drop from the sky, rise out of the snow, and in an instant, we're surrounded by winged figures who wear sapphire blue tunics with a silver insignia in the shape of a snowflake on the breast. I spin in a circle, looking for a gap in their ranks, but find none.

"You are trespassing in the Winter Court," one of the Fae barks. "State your business or risk persecution."

"Aw," Vlad coos. "You must be new."

"Vladimir?" a different male asks, stepping forward. He has pale white hair and gray eyes that swirl like the storm raging around us. His tunic is embroidered with extra silver accents, which I assume means he's the one in charge.

Vlad smiles cockily. "Glad to see someone competent."

"You didn't announce your arrival," the male in charge says. "Queen Gwyneira won't be pleased. You know she likes advance notice."

"I think she'll make an exception." Vlad places his hand on the small of my back and guides me forward. "Allow me to officially introduce her royal highness, Princess Edina of the Winter Court. Fresh from the mortal realm."

"Our princess?" the male gasps, searching my face. "Are you sure?"

"Look at her," Vlad says. The man steps closer, studying me like I'm an animal in a zoo.

"Can we have this conversation inside?" I ask hostilely. "The snow is depressing."

Vlad grimaces but the white-haired guard laughs heartily. "Sounds like Her Majesty too," he says with a chuckle. "Come along." Vlad tosses my bag at the new guard before ushering me closer to the one in charge.

"My name is Bylur, Your Highness," the white-haired Fae says. "I am Captain of the Guard for Queen Gwyneira."

"Edina is fine," I say, straightening my shoulders.

"May I?" He extends his arm and Vlad takes my other as I'm pulled into the familiar sensation of teleporting. The air compresses, squeezing my lungs, but rather than the gray smoke that usually accompanies the Dark Witch teleportation, we're deposited in a flurry of snowflakes.

We land outside a glass castle. Transparent towers rise so high I can't see the tops, and dotted lights from the open windows make it seem like the stars are that much closer to the earth. A thin layer of frost sparkles in the moonlight, giving the impression the entire exterior is made of ice. Maybe it is. The wall that surrounds the castle is made of thick, sober bricks that are dusted in a fresh snowfall. Guards patrol the top, seemingly unaffected by the flurries that fall around them.

Bylur leads us over a drawbridge made of ice that floats over a river that is surprisingly running. Magical lights line the water, changing color and making the water appear purple, then pink, then yellow. The bridge deposits us on a path of cobblestones that wind through a grove of white-barked trees that bear rich, red fruit. The trees closest to the walk are strung with fairy lights, and I think I hear the flutter of wings and light tinkling chatter as we move through them and closer to the palace.

Large white-wooden doors, adorned with silver accents, swing open for us, and Bylur ushers us inside. We pause in a marble hallway lit with hanging candles. It's still drafty, but the presence of solid walls makes me feel a little less on edge. My boots make a squelching sound on the floor until I have the wherewithal to cast a drying spell.

We continue around a corner into a hall decorated with large portraits of people who could be my siblings. Everyone is tall, everyone is blonde, and everyone is wearing white. And everyone in these pictures is stoic, incredibly somber.

I stop by a picture in a delicate silver frame etched with winter flowers. The eight people in the portrait have their backs turned to the camera, showing off an array of pale wings of different sizes and shapes. They all have their arms around each other's waists as they look out over a snow-covered cliffside that leads to a dark azure ocean.

My eye snags on the only woman in the photo, in a pale gauzy sheath dress. Her hair tumbles in soft waves to the small of her back, and there's a crown atop her head, which is resting on the shoulder of the male at her side. I can almost feel their wistful smiles, their love for each other so palpable that it brings tears to my eyes.

Vlad threads his fingers in mine. "You'll meet them in a minute."

With one last look at the photo, I follow Vlad as he tugs me along after Bylur, who has stopped in front of double doors decorated with silver whorls.

"Wait here," Bylur tells us, and he dips inside the room. I tug on the hem of my blue sweater, which Katie cut holes in the back of so my wings could poke out. Suddenly I feel massively underdressed in my leggings and snow boots. I shift from foot to foot, worrying my bottom lip.

"You've got this," Vlad says gently, and the doors swing open.

Chapter Two

THE THRONE ROOM REMINDS me of a cathedral. Large beams made of the white wood arch so high I can barely see their pinnacle. The floors are a pale gray stone that seems to shimmer under the bright white fairy lights that dangle daintily from the rafters. The two walls along the side of the chamber are glass and overlook a different section of the palace grounds. One shows off the white-barked tree that we saw coming in, and the other overlooks thick evergreens dusted so perfectly with snow that it looks like a Christmas card.

The space is filled to the brim with Fae of every shape and size. Some with wings, some with horns...there's even a woman with a mermaid-like tail who is perched in her own glass enclosure of water. Some gasp when I enter, and others immediately stand and bow.

I summon the courage to straight ahead. The back wall is stone save for the giant stained-glass window that I'm sure is beautiful in the daylight. When there's nothing else to look at in the room, I lock eyes with the woman across the expanse. Her mouth is parted, and she stands from her silver throne, which is carved with the same winter flowers from the picture frame. It must be imbued with magic because it emanates soft blue light that sparkles under a layer of sparkly frost.

The queen descends the dais slowly. It's unsettling how alike we look. Her hair is the same golden yellow, but hers is piled on top of her head in a mountain of curls rather than pin-straight. Even with her giant white ballgown, I can tell she's tall and lithe. I'm not quite sure how the aging process works with Fae, but she only looks a few years my senior, not nearly old enough to be my mother. The only thing that separates us is the color of her eyes, which are so bright and brilliant I can see them across the room. They're such a light blue that they almost look white, and they swirl with magic and power.

As soon as her feet touch the sapphire blue carpet, the same color as my eyes, she's flanked by men. A pale hand drifts across her lush lips as she approaches closer. She scans my body and I feel woefully underdressed.

Beside me Vlad dips into a low bow, tugging my hand as he sinks down, indicating I should also bow, but I'm frozen. This is my birth mother.

"Clear the room please," she speaks. Her voice is deep and resonates even though her volume is barely above a whisper. There's a flurry of movement around us as Fae are ushered out of the throne room by an immeasurable number of guards. It takes three men to move the aquarium housing the mermaid. Once everyone is gone, I'm left in the room with two guards, Vlad, the queen, and seven men who stand in a line behind her.

"Thank the goddess," she breathes once they're all gone. Then she turns to Vlad and offers him a small smile that doesn't quite reach her eyes. "And thank you for returning my daughter,

Vladimir. I am in your debt." The last sentence comes out strained.

"Thank you, Your Majesty," Vlad says, rising to his full height and winking at me with mischief in his eyes. The queen sets her eyes back on me, and I finally have the sense to dip to my knees in a bow and cast my eyes to the floor.

"It's a little late for that," she says. I can't tell if she's joking or peeved, but the temperature in the throne room plummets. "When you were born, your fathers and I named you Solara. But I suspect your human parents gave you another name."

"It's Edina," I say with a little more bite than I intended.

Her pale eyebrows arch in surprise. "Edina," she repeats, moving her mouth around my name like she's tasting it.

"Did you say fathers?" I ask, and I swear I see her mouth twitch in the semblance of a smile before it's schooled back to neutrality.

"Yes, fathers." The men behind my mother take a step forward, closer to her. "One of them is your birth father, I suppose, but we decided when we had you not to find out."

She proceeds to list a string of Fae names that there's no way in hell I'll remember, but I follow along the line as she introduces them. Most of the men have similar builds, tall and thin, but some are built thicker, and one is about the height of my best friend, and she's tiny. Their hair colors vary from deep blue to stark white, and they all have wings that I can't really see. My eyes linger over the male who is seventh in line. He has pitch-black hair, but his eyes are the same sapphire as my own. Doesn't take a rocket scientist to figure out who my father is, but that's fine.

"It's nice to meet you all," I say when my mother ends her roll call.

"There will be a test on that later," the man in the fifth spot in line says with a wink. Apparently, dad jokes span realms.

"No there won't be," the man at the front of the line responds.

"Jokes, Astor," Number Five chides. "We went over this in case of our daughter's return."

"Jokes are meant to make one laugh. Edina didn't laugh," Astor says.

"Well," the queen says, effectively ending their bickering. "It appears we have much to do. We will need to get better acquainted, of course. And you'll need immediate lessons in etiquette, that much is clear."

"Actually, I'm not staying," I say, and eight pairs of eyes widen. "I'm here on behalf of Queen Kathryn of the Dark Magic Covens—"

"The only queen you need to concern yourself with is me," the queen says. "I know this must be an adjustment for you. You just emerged. You have new powers you're unaccustomed to. But you belong in Faerie, at my side, preparing to take your place as the Queen of the Winter Court."

A weight settles on my chest like a led balloon. Queen of the Winter Court. I was prepared for the possibility of staying, but I didn't think I'd have to be queen. Aren't Fae immortal? Why would I need to take over for my mother if she's going to live forever?

"No." It's barely a whisper but the room is so quiet everyone can hear. "No, I'm going back home."

I turn on my heels but run face-first into Vlad's rock-hard chest. His hands reach out to steady me, holding my shoulders in place as I struggle to get out of his grasp. "Edina," he murmurs, and I look up into his piercing blue gaze. "Breathe."

I force a breath into my lungs, and as I exhale, a winter wind more powerful than any natural breath is blown out, ruffling Vlad's cloak. He maintains his hold on me as I take several more breaths, and the air around us returns to a normal temperature. He pulls me into a hug, which is not something he's ever done with me before but feels strangely natural. He carefully avoids my wings as he bends down to whisper in my ear. "You have all the power here," he says. "And we need that army. You can do this."

I nod against him and straighten. This time when I push out of his hold, he lets me go. I turn back to my birth mother, who is watching me curiously. "I'm sorry," I say, my voice sounding more formal than it ever has before. "But I was born in the mortal realm, and I can't leave them in their time of need. I need to help my friend on her quest to restore the balance of the Kingdom of Magic."

The Queen rolls her eyes in a gesture that's uncomfortably familiar. "And you want the Unseelie Army to aid your cause," she surmises. "And in return? What do I get?"

I look over at Vlad who nods in encouragement before steeling my spine. "Once everything is settled in the Kingdom of Magic, and they can spare me, I'll come back. Be your princess."

The queen cocks her head to the side, sizing me up. "I'll think it over." My heart sinks. I literally offered her everything she wanted. How could she not take me up on the offer?

"Your Majesty—" Vlad begins but snaps his mouth shut when she glares at him.

"I need to speak to the royalty of the other courts," the queen continues. "The Unseelie typically wish to stay out of the affairs of humans, and I need to decide if it's worth my while to get them to aid your cause. In three days, we will have a ball to celebrate Solara's—"

"Edina," I correct.

"—return to Faerie. In the meantime, you will begin training with tutors in dance, etiquette, history and politics, and magical prowess. It seems your power could rival mine, but you have no control. You'll need it if you are to fight in your friend's war. I will observe your progress and will decide by the ball if I wish to approach the Kings of Fall and Night Court for use of the Unseelie army."

It doesn't sound like a negotiation, but I know better. So, I nod. Three days is roughly six weeks in the mortal realm. I hope Katie can hang on that long, but if I'm here I can push the queen to hopefully give me an answer faster.

"It's been a long evening," the man second in line says. "Perhaps we should retire, my queen."

"Yes," she says. "You will begin at first light, so I suggest you get some rest. Vladimir, are you staying for the ball?"

"I'm afraid I must leave before daylight," Vlad offers smoothly and zips forward to place a kiss on my mother's hand. "I'll just see that Her Highness is settled in her room so I can report back to my queen and then I'll be off."

"She's your queen as well?" She arches an eyebrow. "I thought vampires avoid witches since the last disaster of a war."

"Typically, we do." Vlad smirks. "But this one is worth standing beside. The werewolves and vampires have pledged our loyalty to her."

My mother tuts and turns to leave. "Your Majesty," Vlad interjects, causing her to halt. "I'd like to call in my favor."

"Name it," she says through gritted teeth, her giant skirts swishing around as she faces Vlad once more.

"I'd like to take the palace healer back with me for one evening in the mortal realm."

My eyebrows scrunch as I look at Vlad, but he gives nothing else away. "What could you possibly need with Eirwen?" my mother asks.

"I need his evaluation and potential healing for a friend."

"Fine," she says and nods to one of the guards. "He'll be waiting here when you leave."

"Thank you." Without another word, my mother leaves out the far end of the throne room, her men crowding around her.

"The vampires are standing with Katie?" I breathe, low enough that I hope the guards don't hear. "I thought you needed to convene a council."

"Technically," Vlad says. "But they'll agree with me. I'm a big deal, Tinker Bell."

"But Katie doesn't know that."

Vlad laughs, a low and throaty sound that's barely audible. "Watching her squirm is my new hobby. Immortality can be dull without ways to entertain yourself. You'll see."

Chapter Three

THE REMAINING GUARDS LEAD us out of the throne room through a door that's hidden amidst the stonework on the back wall.

I'm in a fog as we traipse through the palace. Everything is a blur of white and silver, but I can't focus on the details. The walls feel like they're closing in. The staircases make me dizzy. The neckline of my sweater is too high, and I'm somehow too hot and too cold all at once.

Vlad links his arm through mine and squeezes, anchoring me enough that I can keep control of my magic.

It feels like hours before the guards stop before a non-descript door in a non-descript hallway. One male turns the knob, pushing it inward and slipping inside. I go to follow, but Vlad uses the slightest pressure on my arm to keep me still. The guard emerges, giving us the all-clear, and Vlad tugs me into the room, shutting the door behind us.

The room is...not a room. It's a fucking mansion tucked inside the palace. The door opens into a formal sitting room that has three doorways. I can't even see all the rooms attached, but I can see a dining room, a bathroom, what looks like a library, a dance studio, and finally, the bedroom that has a second bathroom. It's a lot. Too much.

I pace the length of the sitting room, walking from the door to the white brick fireplace that's lit with a roaring fire. Why is everything in this court white? I'm all for embracing a brand, but I'm afraid to touch anything, that I'll tarnish the pristine surfaces. Vlad takes off his shoes, and I follow suit, kicking off my boots before I resume pacing.

"You have to calm down." He sounds almost bored as he takes off his cloak, revealing the full three-piece suit underneath before flopping down on the white fainting couch closest to the fire.

"Are you kidding me?" My voice hits a decibel only dogs can hear. "I'm in a world I know nothing about, and the fate of my world depends on me becoming the perfect princess. I know you haven't known me very long, but I'm no princess. I'm loud and crass and I have serious issues with authority. And I swear to god—"

"Goddess," Vlad amends. "They worship a goddess here."

"SEE?" I squeal. Wind picks up around me, whipping through the room and making the fire dance as the flames struggle to remain lit. "I can't do this. I should leave with you. We'll be fine without Fae soldiers, right?"

"No, we won't." Vlad stands and blocks my path around the sitting room. "Edina, look at me." I have to crane my neck to look into his eyes, which is impressive because I'm tall. He crowds in closer, so close that when I take in a deep breath our chests touch. "What do you need?"

"I need to get out of here—"

"No. What do you need to calm down?"

Honestly, it's not healthy, but when I'm feeling less than in other aspects of my life, I look for a physical distraction. A shot of serotonin. Something to take me out of my brain. I used to swim, but somewhere along the way, I found a better alternative. But I can't ask that of Vlad. I make it a point to keep my sex life and my personal life separate. And even though we just met, I know in my bones that Vlad is going to be a part of my life. My immortal life. No, this would be a terrible idea.

Then again, when have I ever turned down a terrible idea?

"Nothing you can help me with," I respond. Vlad nods, taking a step back, only to halt when my hand grips the lapel of his jacket. "Nothing you should help me with."

I look up at him through my lashes. Vlad smiles knowingly and backs me against the door. One hand falls to my hip, while the other brushes a stray piece of hair behind my ear before cupping the back of my neck possessively. Up close, I take a moment to appreciate how gorgeous Vlad is. He looks like an old-Hollywood movie star with his slicked-back hair and his strong jaw. And he has that air about him that screams I'm good at sex. I mean he has been alive a long time, it would be depressing if he didn't know how to fuck.

"Is this what you want?" he asks, tugging me so our bodies are flush against each other. "Release?"

"Yes," I breathe. "But—"

"I can separate sex from emotions, princess. It won't be awkward between us."

"It's a one-time thing," I confirm. "What happens in Faerie and all that."

"If that's what you want." His head tilts down just far enough that his breath tickles my lips. "I'm gonna need a safe word."

"Watermelon," I respond without thinking.

"Any hard limits? Kinks I should know about?"

"Nothing in my ass, and don't bite me." I shift closer. "You?"

"I'm immortal, princess, nothing's off-limits."

"Don't call me princess," I say, taking hold of both sides of his jacket. "I don't want to be reminded of reality right now."

I press up on my toes and gently nip at his bottom lip. His resounding growl reverberates through me. I'm not sure who closes the distance first, but our lips collide frantically. There's nothing slow or romantic about this. It's carnal, a way to work off some anxious energy.

I flick my tongue along one extended fang as I slide his jacket off his shoulders. "I suggest you stay away from those if you don't want me to bite you." Vlad's hands find the holes in the back of my sweater and there's a satisfying rip as he shreds the material so it falls off in a pool of fabric.

I undo the clasp on my bra and toss it to the side as Vlad's tongue trails a line down my neck directly to my breast. He sucks my nipple into his mouth, and I throw my head back, my long hair brushing against the small of my back.

Vlad doesn't linger. It's like he knows I don't need a lot of foreplay. He probably does. I can scent his arousal as he sinks to his knees in front of me and yanks my leggings and thong off in one go. Something about him being mostly clothed and me being completely naked is so hot I can't even form words. His eyes connect with mine for a long blink before he runs his tongue up the length of my slit.

"Fuck, E," he hums. "Already so wet for me." I sigh as he seals his lips around my clit, and his fangs brush against the sensitive bundle of nerves just enough that it has me squirming against him.

"Vlad," I plead as he sinks a finger inside me and instantly finds my g-spot. "There is one thing I like. I just don't tell a lot of people about it."

"Mmm," he responds, not removing his mouth from my clit as his finger begins pumping in and out of me.

"I–" My own guttural moan breaks off my statement. "Oh god, don't stop."

"Goddess," Vlad murmurs, and I grip his hair and force him back between my legs. He chuckles and at the same time adds a second finger, and the combination of the fullness and the vibrations sends me over the edge. I keep a hold of his hair as I thrust my hips forward, riding his face even as my legs grow weak.

Vlad coaxes me through my orgasm and then slowly rises to his full height. "Couch, now," he orders.

"Yes, vampire daddy," I chide, and as I turn, he smacks my ass...hard.

"Is that your thing?" he croons, pushing me over the arm of the couch so my ass is in the air. He rubs away the hurt as he grinds his hard cock against me. "Are you a brat?"

"No." I chuckle. "Well probably...but I don't have a daddy kink."

"Pity." I try to push myself up, but Vlad grabs my hands and holds them behind my back. "Bondage?" he asks, switching both of my wrists into one of his large hands, leaving me completely at his mercy.

"Nope." The sound of Vlad's zipper sliding down has me biting my lip in anticipation. "It's—"

"Don't tell me," he orders, dragging his cock up my sex from my entrance to my clit. I whimper as he repeats the motion. "I want to guess."

He slams into me, and I cry out, faceplanting into the couch. Fuck, he's huge. Even warmed up, it takes my body a second to get used to his girth. He holds still, allowing my body to adjust until I nod.

"What's your safe word?" he says, his voice gritty and rough around the edges.

"Watermelon."

"Good girl." He starts moving inside me, slowly sliding back out before slamming into me again. It's slow enough to be teasing but hard enough to have me building to another climax.

"You gonna guess my kink, or am I just telling you so you can get me off?" I taunt.

Vlad drops his hold on my hands and takes a large handful of my hair, tugging so hard he lifts me. My back is arched against his chest as he starts to pick up his pace. In this position, my clit is rubbing against the soft material of the couch and it has me squirming.

"Let's see," Vlad says, slowing his pace enough that I growl. "You didn't want me to bite you, so nothing too primal." His free hand slips around my hips, settling between my legs as he gently draws circles around my clit. "You didn't respond to the 'good girl,' so it's not a praise kink."

My laugh turns to a breathy moan as he pinches my clit and slams inside me in the same motion. "Degradation?" he asks.

"I swear to god—"

"Goddess."

"—if you call me a slut, I will freeze your dick off."

"No degradation for you then." He laughs and starts fucking me harder. His pace becomes punishing and draws a string of profanity from my lips. "You don't tell a lot of people, which either means it's something you're embarrassed about or it's dangerous."

I swear as he pulls out and turns me around, studying me, even as his fingers keep working my clit. "You're not the type to get embarrassed."

I stare into his eyes, and his pupils dilate as the realization crashes over him. "Oh, Edina," he tsks. With strength that shouldn't be possible, he lifts me from the couch and lowers us to the ground, not wasting a second before sliding back inside me. He grips one ankle, throwing it over his shoulder and the new position has him hitting so deep my eyes roll back in my head.

"I'm not into orgasm denial, Vlad," I pant. "Make me fucking come already."

He chuckles darkly, rising up to his knees for a second before one hand circles my throat. My breath catches and my pulse increases beneath his fingers. "There it is." He smirks, his fangs fully extended. "Tap my arm twice if you want this to stop, understand?"

"Yes," I breathe. I thought Vlad was fucking me hard before. But holy shit, it's nothing compared to what he does when he's losing control. His movements are so fast I can barely breathe. It's brutal in a way that will lead to a delicious hurt tomorrow.

His hand stays on my throat, applying light pressure until I'm quickly approaching orgasm. "Vlad," I plead. His fingers squeeze the sides of my neck, cutting off my air. I'm right there, teetering over the edge of a cliff. My vision starts to blur, stars burst in front of my eyes.

He lets up on the pressure and I take a large breath as my orgasm crashes through me. I'm freefalling. There's nothing in this world but the pleasure that has a hold of my body. My back arches off the ground, my mouth open in a silent scream. My inner walls grip Vlad's cock, and he pumps twice more before he spills inside me with a roar loud enough to rattle the gray-scale pictures on the walls.

Vlad rolls off, flopping onto the floor beside me as our chests heave and we desperately try to get our breathing under control. "Fuck, that was hot," I say, my voice husky and a bit raw.

"Yeah, it was," Vlad agrees, before standing and gathering me into his arms.

"What the hell are you doing?" I ask as he carries me to the giant four-poster bed. He pushes aside the white canopy, tossing the fur comforter down before laying me in the dead center.

"It's called aftercare, Tinker Bell," he replies with a smirk. I roll my eyes but stay still as he zips into the attached bathroom and returns with a damp washcloth.

"Please tell me there's running water in this realm," I plead as Vlad starts to clean me up.

"There is."

"Thank the goddess," I murmur, overemphasizing the deity and making Vlad laugh heartily. He finishes his ministrations and zooms back to the bathroom to clean himself up. He returns in less than a minute, still fully dressed, and slides into bed with me. "What do you think you're doing?"

"Shut up and come here," he says, extending his arm back on the pillows in invitation.

"I don't cuddle," I say, even as he uses his superior strength to tug me into his side.

"I've seen you cuddle Katie."

"That's different," I murmur as my head falls onto his chest. "She's the exception."

"Well, when I choke you, I'm the other exception," he says.

"That was a one-time thing."

"Sure." He chuckles as I settle into his hold. He starts rubbing the spot between my wings and I groan as it releases the knot that's been back there since I emerged.

"Do you have to leave soon?"

"Yes," he says. I nod, my eyes heavy as I feel sleep already starting to claim me.

"Tell Katie I love her," I murmur. "I hate that I won't be able to talk to her. There's no way to communicate between realms, right?"

"The only way is through a two-way mirror," Vlad answers.

"Seriously?" I sit up and summon my bag, which knocks the doors of a wooden wardrobe open on its trek. I dig around until I find the inside pocket that holds a necklace with two charms. I slide one off before fastening the chain around my neck. Vlad regards me curiously as I wave my hand over the charm until it expands to its original size, revealing a handheld mirror. The glass is old and clouded on the edges, but the silver backing is still resplendent with its swirling snowflake pattern.

I hold the mirror out to Vlad. "Tell her I'll call her in the morning my time."

"Why do you have that?" Vlad asks.

"I found the pair of mirrors in an oddities shop in Salem and thought it was cooler than FaceTime. More witchy. I barely used mine once I learned how to enchant regular mirrors, but I always keep it on this necklace just in case."

"I'll give it to her," he says. Vlad leans over and kisses my cheek. "I have to go before daylight."

I swallow the lump in my throat as I nod, holding the comforter up over my naked body. Vlad stands, smoothing down his wrinkle-free pants, before turning back to me. "You can do this, Tinker Bell."

I laugh, and Vlad smiles at the sound. "Thanks for the orgasms," I say, causing him to laugh in earnest. "Now get out."

Vlad winks and leaves my chambers. As the door clicks shut, my smile fades and my fears resurface. I flop back on the pillows and pray to the goddess I know nothing about to keep my mind quiet until sleep claims me.

Chapter Four

"WE NEED TO WAKE her," a female voice hisses, drawing me from sleep.

"You do it," another voice says.

"No, you!"

I crack one eye open and release a puff of air to blow the hair from my face. Hovering above my head are two figures no larger than the size of a dragonfly. They both have silvery wings that flutter so quickly I can barely keep track of the beats. Their bodies are lithe, and they each wear what appear to be dresses made for dolls. The only difference between the otherwise identical creatures is their hair, one is a bright magenta, and the other a deep royal purple.

The one with the magenta hair slaps the other across the arm. "You woke her!" she bellows in a voice far louder than should be possible from such a small body. Purple hair's face turns a brilliant shade of red and she launches at the other.

I watch them tussle for a bit, giving myself a moment to wake up from what I'm sure is a dream until I remember where I am. The windows have been thrown open, and the early morning light reveals the pristine white room with delicate silver accents. I clutch the fur comforter closer as I drink in everything from the tall glass mirror atop a white vanity, to the oversized wardrobe with a swirling snowflake pattern decorated on the side. The Winter Court is really on the nose with its aesthetic.

I'm genuinely considering drawing the gossamer curtains over the bed and going back to sleep, but I made a promise to Katie, so I can't just wallow. I've never been homesick, but that's the closest I can come to describing this feeling. It's an intense desire to leave this frozen hell and return to a world where I fit in.

Except I don't fit there anymore. I have wings and pointed ears and magic that blasts out at the least provocation. And if I don't fit in Faerie or the mortal realm...then I don't fit in anywhere.

The creatures in my room stop fighting and turn back to me in a state of disarray. Magenta waves her hand over the both of them, righting their clothing while Purple fixes their hair and removes all manner of bruises and welts.

"So sorry, Your Highness," Magenta says. "My name is Althea, and this is Brigid."

Brigid smiles brightly. "We're your lady's maids."

"Nice to meet you." They both smile widely, revealing delicately pointed teeth. "I'm sorry this is rude, but what are you?"

Their laughter is in perfect harmony. "We're Pixies, Your Majesty," Althea says, tossing her magenta hair over her shoulder.

"And it's not rude at all," Brigid responds quickly. "We know you grew up in the mortal realm and are unaware of everything that Faerie has to offer. We don't mind helping."

"Though your fathers will start your lessons this afternoon."

"After your dress fitting and breakfast with your mother." Brigid claps her small hands. When I don't move, she and Althea fly on either side of me and tug my arms. They're crazy strong, and they push and pull until I'm standing, still completely naked.

"What the hell—" I start, but they simply fly to my shoulders and guide me to the vanity. Althea flies to my head and pushes down until I plop in the seat as Brigid goes to the wardrobe, throwing open the double doors and returning with a white silk robe.

"No need to get dressed since the seamstress will be here in a moment," she says, tossing the robe at me. "But there's also no reason to flaunt everything the goddess gave you."

"Modesty is expected of all royals," Althea instructs. "Except in private, naturally."

"Speaking of..." Brigid and Althea start buzzing around my head, combing out my hair. "How was Vlad last night? Was he as good as we've heard?"

"Both the males and the females of this realm are quite excited whenever he arrives." Althea pins a curl on top of my head as I finally get a second to slide my arms into the robe and hastily tie it. My wings unfurl through dainty slits in the back.

"The size difference is the only thing that's held us back," Brigid continues. "But I wonder if there's a way we could—"

I don't get to answer or ask how they knew I was with Vlad. Their gossip comes at warp speed and is full of so many names and places I know nothing of that they might as well be speaking another language. It makes my head pound.

The Pixies make quick work of my hair, piling it into a crown of curls atop my head, and even though I wrinkle my nose at the style, I never get the chance to protest.

A knock at the door is the only thing that halts their chatter. Althea goes to the door, only to be blasted aside as it's thrown open. She tumbles in the air, shaking her colorful head and scowling at the Fae who enters.

"Melia," Althea squeals, her face turning red again.

"Buzz off." Melia waves the Pixie away like she's a bothersome insect. She's a short creature, the top of her head only reaching the doorknob. Her unruly black curls are fighting to escape their tie, a complete contradiction to the impossibly clean and pressed white tunic she wears. Brown eyes that match the warm rich color of her skin appraise me, eying me from head to toe.

"Are you the seamstress?" I ask, and Melia huffs.

"She is." Brigid pins the last of my hair and moves to my shoulder to prod me up.

"Let's go, Your Highness," Melia barks, moving back into the sitting room. She snaps her stubby fingers and procures a pedestal and several tape measures.

"Did you just pull that out of the fucking air?" I gape at the seamstress because *she just pulled that out of the fucking air.*

"Most Fae can manifest items," Althea says as Melia taps her foot impatiently and I step onto the pedestal. "Ask your fathers today, I'm sure they'll show you."

Melia works quickly, helped by the Pixies who zip around catching the tape measures that Melia throws around my body. She scratches measurements in a notebook that she also *manifests* from thin air. I seriously need to learn to do that.

When they're done measuring my head—for my tiara, naturally—Melia snaps her fingers again and produces an array of blue velvets, ranging from light to dark.

"Pick," her rough voice commands.

"Oh." I inspect the material. "I'm not really a velvet fan—"

"Pick."

I huff, wondering if I can pull rank, before deciding it's not worth the hassle and pointing at the powder blue one on the far end. Melia nods and replaces the fabric with sketches of ballgowns. And I mean ballgowns. None of those A-line, mermaid, or trumpet styles. All the sketches have full skirts and corseted tops. The only difference, that I can see, is in the bodice. Some are sweetheart shaped, while others have a high neckline and are completely covered.

"Absolutely not." I snatch the pen from Melia's hands and pick the least offensive dress. Over the top of the monstrosity pictured, I draw a silhouette that will flow and not draw attention to my lack of boobs or an ass but will still show some of my body. I leave the off-the-shoulder look but add in a deep v down to the small of my back. "That," I instruct.

The seamstress laughs and snaps her fingers, removing all the ink from my drawing so it's back to its original sketch. "That," she agrees with a sneer.

"No." I take a step closer to Melia, but she holds her ground, making me crane my neck down as I tower over her. Ice coats the knuckles of my balled fists.

"Your Highness, this is the style in the Winter Court," Althea steps in. "The style you requested is more in line with Summer or Spring and would be considered..."

"Inappropriate," Brigid offers.

"Yes, inappropriate." I roll my eyes and acquiesce, picking the same design since I'm clearly not getting a choice. They can put me in a trash bag for all I care.

Melia chuckles tauntingly, and everything she brought into the room disappears. She holds out her hand and waits.

"Thank you?" I tentatively reach for her hand to shake it.

"No," Althea screams, making me jerk my hand back. "You need to give her payment. She's a Brownie, so anything but clothing."

"What?" I balk, looking at the Pixies. "I don't have anything—"

"Your necklace perhaps?" Brigid asks as Althea flies to the back of my neck to unclasp the chain.

"No." The necklace was a gift from Katie. It's not worth anything, but it's the only thing I have that's tethering me back to home, to my real family.

My magic clearly decides that it's had enough and takes this moment to show up and blast the three Fae away in a torrent of icy wind. The Pixies tumble, grasping the couch in the sitting room for support as the Brownie just stares me down, her black curls the only thing that's movable.

I take a deep breath, willing my magic to recede in my veins. When I rein it in, there's a blast radius of ice around me. The Brownie gives me a pitying look and sets about cleaning up my mess, scooping broken glass from the pictures I knocked off the wall and righting displaced furniture.

"Not the necklace," I say to Althea and Brigid when they fly back over to me. "What else can I give her?"

"We brought a tea tray in this morning in case you woke earlier," Brigid offers, albeit much more cautiously. "There's a jar of honey from the Spring Court—"

"Fine." She nods and flies into what I assume is a dining room.

The door to the suite explodes open, and a tall Fae storms in. He's scarily pale, his eyebrows and eyelashes almost blending into his papery skin, and his wings look like bat wings...if bat wings were white and sparkly. He scans the room, regarding the ice spreading along the floor around me.

"Everything's fine, Eirwen," Althea says to the man. "No one's hurt."

Eirwen ignores them and looks at me. "Princess. You need to call Kathryn immediately."

"What's wrong? What happened?"

"I'm not at liberty to discuss my patients, even with you, Your Highness," he says, bowing at the waist. When he straightens, he stares at me for an uncomfortable amount of time.

"Am I supposed to give him honey too?" I ask the Pixies. Eirwen huffs, and storms from the room. I don't know how the fuck I offended him, but apparently, that's par for the course this morning. "I need a minute."

"You have to meet with your mother for—"

"I. Need. A. Minute." Both Pixies shut up as I leave the sitting area and go back to the vanity in my bedroom. I cast the spell over the mirror, and the glass fogs over, dark gray on the edges and lighter towards the middle. Slowly, the color shifts and the picture comes into focus...on a close-up of cleavage. I can't help the laugh that bubbles up.

"As much as I've missed your tits, I'd much rather see your face."

Katie shrieks, bursting my eardrums in the most amazing way possible. She pulls the mirror away from her boobs, and her face fills the frame, providing me instant comfort. Her chestnut hair is tied up in a messy bun, and the bags under her auburn eyes give away how tired she is.

"Are you trying to kill me?" she cackles. I join in her laughter but it's bordering on tears. Naturally, she sees right through my façade. "What's wrong?"

"I miss you so fucking much," I squeak.

I open my mouth to tell her everything that's happened so far. That I'm homesick, that they want to train me to take over the throne. That I might have to move here permanently, and I can't deal with it. And that even though I've offered everything I have, the Fae still might not help us.

But then I hear the sound of wings fluttering and feet treading too close to the door to my room.

"Can I have the room please?" I ask the unseen lurkers. Althea grumbles under her breath, and Melia growls before stomping to the door of my suite and slamming it shut behind the three of them. I hold up a finger for Katie to wait until I hear their conversation dissipate in the hallway.

When I'm sure they're gone, I turn my attention back to my best friend. "I should be asking you what's wrong. Some dude name Eirwen stormed in here and told me I need to call you immediately. And then he acted like I owed him a fucking favor for telling me."

"My magic is fucked," she says. "But I'm okay right now. Lowell and Vlad helped."

"Is that your way of telling me you had a threesome?" Her laughter is like a balm for my soul, and I join her, but my heart isn't in it.

"Tell me about Faerie," she insists.

"I haven't seen much." I opt to leave out the fact that Vlad and I fucked in case I was right about the threesome thing. "It's all ice and snow and people to match. I asked about soldiers fighting with us, but they gave me the runaround. I'll try again today."

"You can come home if it's too much."

"No. I'll be fine. I grew up on the Upper East Side. I know how to handle ruthless people who smile in your face while trying to stab you in the back."

"Well fuck," she breathes. "Are you sure?"

No. "Yeah." I change the topic quickly. "So, if the wolf and vampire daddy helped you–" I wink, "–why do you look upset?"

She sighs and says it's nothing, but I know that sigh. It's her avoidance sigh. I arch my eyebrow and wait.

"My father tried to overthrow me twice today. Oh, and Adriana's new clairvoyance teacher is Rodger...who apparently only broke up with me because he kept seeing all the ways I would die. But that didn't stop him from appearing naked on my bed tonight spouting some psychological bullshit about how I hate being alone."

"Huh," I muse. That's not the full story. She's not upset about the fact that her ex is there. "And that's bothering you because you're considering sleeping with the wolf."

"No," she sputters. Bullseye. "I'm not..."

"Mhmm." I flatten my mouth into a line. "Okay, so two things. One...Rodger is a fuckwit."

"Accurate."

"Two," I sigh heavily. "How many times have you almost died in the past year? Hell, the last week."

"Where are you going with this?" she asks.

"My point is, if you don't want to be alone, don't be alone. Especially not when there's a hot-as-fuck werewolf who wants to be the one to keep you company."

Because seriously, I would have hit that like four times over already. Okay, that's a lie. I would have hit it once and then peaced out after. But I'm sure it would have been amazing...that wolf has big dick energy and the goods to back it up. Not that I would ever say that out loud because Katie seems all kinds of territorial over him.

"What about the necklace?" she asks softly, and I fight the urge to roll my eyes. Her other psycho ex gave her a gaudy heart-shaped necklace and claimed—because it magically mimicked a heartbeat when she put it on—that he was her true love. Total bullshit if you ask me.

"I would be honest with Lowell about it," I say carefully. "And for all you know it's my heartbeat you're hearing."

"That would make things so much easier." She laughs. "Do Fae have true loves? Or mates or whatever?"

"Yes," I say too harshly. I don't want to think about potentially finding a mate here. It seems so...permanent. "I have to go soon, babes, but can I ask a favor before I do?"

"Always."

"Can you call my parents?" I ask. "Tell them what's going on? It's the New Year there, right? They'll worry when I don't show up for my last semester." They probably haven't noticed I'm missing-- we don't spend Christmases together-- but as soon as the semester starts they'll get a phone call.

"I'll take care of it," she assures me. "The second things get too hard there, you come straight home. I'll tell Vlad to leave the portal open for you."

"Okay." Tears are already brimming in my eyes at the thought of ending this conversation. "Love you."

"Love you most," she says, and I remove the spell from the mirror. I sigh heavily, staring at my reflection with my ridiculous hairstyle and my vacant eyes.

"You can come out now," I call, and the Pixies fly in right away.

"We weren't listening," Brigid assures me.

"We just need to get you ready for breakfast with your mother," Althea adds. I click my tongue, but stand and hold my arms out, waiting for them to dress me.

Chapter Five

THE ATRIUM LOOKS LIKE an igloo if an igloo was made of glass with silver panes that lie in perfect squares. It's surrounded by a grove of evergreens, and light snow cascades off the glass in gentle flurries before adding to the iridescent ground.

"Did you enjoy your fitting?" my birth mother asks from across the long table. She's gently stirring her tea, the sound of her spoon clinking against the side of her china cup. Her expression is stoic. Pleasant, but not warm. Her hair is more elaborate than mine, her curls piled high within a silver crown. She's in a similar, but smaller version of the dress she wore yesterday, white and elaborate, but not quite as full.

"Not really," I answer honestly, knowing she would have heard of my outburst. I fidget with the long sleeves of my dress, another velvet monstrosity that's so heavy I can barely move and covers up almost every inch of my skin.

"Melia said you wanted to wear something more..." She doesn't finish the sentence but her nose scrunches.

"Ballgowns aren't really my style." I take a pointed sip of my bland tea and we continue to stare in silence.

I reach for the plate of pastries closest to me, but it slides back just as my hand grazes a cookie. "Princesses don't lean across the table," my mother says. "Wait to be served or use your magic."

I roll my eyes but summon two scones and a cookie. I bite into the latter, devouring the whole thing in two bites and making her ice eyes narrow.

"May I ask a question?"

"Sure," I say amidst a mouth of crumbs.

"My guards overheard talk that you've been to Faerie before." Her eyes are practically dilated in excitement.

"That's not a question."

"Who brought you here? And which court did you visit?"

"Why do you want to know?" She sighs like I'm tedious, but that's fine. I'd rather be tedious than admit too much and get someone in trouble.

"Because if I'm correct," she says carefully, "and you were in the Spring Court with Puck, that could be considered an act of war."

Well, shit. She nods as if my silence is an answer. "Did he take you to Titania?"

"We went to his house."

"A palace?"

"It was a treehouse and I mocked him mercilessly for it." I smile at the memory, then immediately try to hide it. "Then he told me he suspected I was Fae and asked me to stay. I told him he was out of his mind and said no. So he brought me back to the portal and that was that."

She cocks her head to the side. "You're defensive when it comes to him."

"Not particularly." I shrug. "He was a good fuck."

"Must you be so crass?"

"I grew up in New York." I doubt she understands what that means, but she sighs and takes a delicate bite of a scone.

"Tell me about your *adoptive* parents." The word *adoptive* is said like a curse.

"There's nothing to tell," I respond, remembering Vlad's earlier warning.

"Nothing? You spent twenty-one years with them—"

"I went to boarding school. So I only saw them for holidays and summers." Her eyebrows raise and her tongue clicks. "Magical boarding schools are pretty common in the mortal realm—"

"I'm just surprised," she says, ire coating her words. "Why go to the trouble of stealing a child—"

"They didn't steal me," I growl. My hands grip the edge of the table, my knuckles turning white. "It was a man. He was killed by the magical army when they discovered he'd been selling changelings."

"Then they purchased you." Her face is still impassive, but her voice wavers and makes the air tremble with power. "As I was saying, why go to the trouble of purchasing a child only to ship them off to boarding school?"

I don't answer. I've already given her too much, but her words feel like a blow to the gut. My fingers loosen, and I try not to let her see the doubt radiating in my chest.

"How about friends?" my mother asks. "Any of those in the mortal realm? A boyfriend, perhaps?"

I scoff. "I'm not really the commitment type."

"That's because you haven't met your fated mate. Hopefully, that will change at the ball."

"Excuse me?" She sips her tea without taking her eyes off me. "I thought the ball was to introduce me to the Fae society."

"And to find your mate, if they're alive, that is." *Nope, hard pass.* I've barely spent an entire night with someone, I have no desire to spend my immortal life with one person. Fae. *Whatever.*

"I'm not interested in a mate," I say firmly. "What I *am* interested in is getting your army to help my Kingdom."

"Your Kingdom is here." There's no hint of anger or emotion in her voice. It's like she's stating a fact about the weather. Frost seeps from my fingertips, inching onto the scone in my hand. "Suppress that," she instructs, her shrewd eyes not missing a thing.

"I don't know how," I grit through my teeth.

"Breathe. When untrained, your magic responds to your emotions."

"No shit."

"Enough." Her voice echoes off the glass and storm clouds dance across her eyes. "Take a deep breath and let your magic release." I do as she says, putting thoughts of staying in this realm aside. The ice in my veins recedes and the temperature of the room warms.

"You'd do well to remember," my mother says as she retakes her seat, "that I am not only your mother but your queen."

"I apologize Your Majesty," I sneer.

"Your apology is accepted." It takes me a minute to realize she missed the sarcasm dripping from every word. "But Mother is fine."

I swallow my rising jab. I need to be levelheaded if I'm going to get this army in time for Katie. It's already been over a week back home; I need to expedite this process. "Mother," I start. She gives me a small smile, her features softening. "You asked about friends I had in the mortal realm."

"Yes."

"I'm not sure if you know, but being Fae in the Kingdom of Magic is dangerous. Most are killed on sight."

"I'm aware," she says solemnly. "Whenever we send scouts, they must retract their wings and glamour their ears."

"You can retract your wings?" That would have been fucking handy days ago. Before we got into this mess.

"Your fathers will teach you."

I nod my thanks before continuing, keeping my tone even. "My best friend, Kathryn, risked everything by taking me to the Dark Witches. While we were there, she had to swear allegiance to them in exchange for keeping me safe. She vowed to lead them in a war to right the balance in the Kingdom, and to hopefully make it safe for Fae to return to the mortal realm."

"While that is a positive," my mother says, "it won't be enough to sway the other courts to surrender their forces. Not when the Seelie are poised to attack."

"They are?"

"They always are." She sips her tea. "Your friend doesn't sound convinced she even wants this war."

I sigh heavily. "She didn't. Not until she was attacked with hellfire."

My mother's skin goes pale. "You're sure it was hellfire?"

"You can ask Eirwen, he examined her. I'm surprised he didn't tell you the second he got back."

"Your fathers and I were occupied, so I sent him away," she says, and that's enough information for me. Although I'm kind of curious how that works with seven of them. There seems to be a disproportionate number of poles to holes.

My mother snaps her fingers and two Pixies, with two shades of blue hair, appear at her side. She murmurs something to them, and they nod emphatically before disappearing.

"This changes things," she announces. "I will speak to the Unseelie Courts and inform them of this new development. In the meantime, it's time for your lessons with your fathers."

With a wave of her hand, the entire tea setup disappears, including the table. "Olwen will teach you the etiquette that will be expected of you for the ball. He'll be along shortly." She stands, giving me a curt nod, before she exits the atrium, guards falling in behind her.

I AM LITERALLY READY to tear my hair out.

"Again," Astor calls, and I glare at him, trying to turn my gaze into a death ray. It doesn't work.

"They never tell you in movies how much the training montage sucks," I grumble while rolling my shoulders.

Astor cocks his head to the side, confusion darkening his navy eyes. "Training montage?"

"It's..." I sigh heavily. "It'll never translate, forget it." Of my fathers, Astor is by far the most literal. It doesn't stop me from using sarcasm in every sentence, but it's infinitely more frustrating.

I take my place across from him. We're in a clearing not far from the atrium where my mother and I had tea. The small patch of snow-covered land is completely surrounded by thick evergreens that grow so close that there's almost no path. I assume it's not an issue for the Fae who can fly, but as evident from the past two days, that's not me.

I brush aside the wisps of hair that have escaped my braid and stand in the center with Astor as he beats his white wings. I try to mimic his movements, but my wings are flapping too fast. I hover off the ground, but I have no control. My body starts to spin as I try to correct my motion and only one wing seems to get the idea.

"ARGH," I scream as I tumble from the sky and onto my shoulder in a giant heap.

Astor flutters down beside me, brushing a non-existent stray hair back into place. "You're not getting better," he observes.

"No shit," I sneer as I right myself, stretching my already sore shoulder. Thankfully this time it didn't pop out of place.

"Your other fathers have said you've shown great progress in those lessons."

I think that's supposed to be a compliment, but I'm not sure, so I don't respond. He's right though; I am getting better in all other aspects of my training. Magic, under any circumstances, is tied to emotion. But I've learned that the more I use it when my emotions are running high, the harder it will be to control. I've been working really hard on clearing my mind before I cast, and it's been helping. My magic now is essentially a stronger version of what I've always had, so once I mastered control, the rest was easy. Except for manifesting items...that's a bitch to learn.

"Humans aren't meant to fly," I mutter under my breath.

"You're not human." I blink up at Astor from where I sit in the snow.

I'm not human.

I've never been human. I'm a completely different species.

I don't know how to unpack that.

"Try again," Astor says, softer this time. "Trust your instincts. It's in your blood."

He extends a hand, and I take it, allowing him to help me to my feet. Assuming the position Astor taught me for take-off, I release a long breath and imagine myself flying out of the clearing. I imagine the kiss of the winter wind on my skin, in my hair.

"Open your eyes, Princess," Astor calls.

I'm above the trees, hovering fifty feet above the clearing. The thin air rushes into my lungs and it feels like the first deep breath I've taken in weeks. Like I've been underwater for too long. The fear fades to exhilaration. The doubt changes to awe. The tension in my body disappears as I lean into instinct.

I was made for this.

I feel stronger in the air, like the source of my power lies a hundred feet above the ground. The cold swirls around me and my wings react, spinning me with it. They have a mind of their own, knowing what to do even though I can't name the movements.

I whoop, pumping my fist in the air, and do a backflip that thankfully doesn't send me to the ground. Astor chuckles beside me, and after my celebration, says, "Look at your court, Princess."

I take the invitation to start flying in wide circles. My wings switch from gentle fluttering to large sweeps, and I angle my body in the direction I want to go. Astor stays behind me, far enough to give me space, but close enough that he can help if I need him. The air current takes me east, where the evergreens give way to charcoal-gray rocks. The ground abruptly drops off as I dip lower, and I'm hit by the salty spray of the ocean that crashes against the rocks at the bottom of a cliff. I laugh as I pull back up, taking in the azure ocean that spreads as far as the eye can see.

"This is your mother's favorite place," Astor says, his voice carrying across the winter wind. A head breaches the water, the creature tipping its head to the sunlight. They wave a hand that ends in black barbs when they see us, and I return the gesture before spinning around and heading back to shore.

I fly over the small village to the north, staying high in the air so I'm not seen by the Fae that mill about the cobblestone streets. I don't bother with the wasteland to the south; I already walked through it and am not eager to return.

"Let's go this way," Astor says, turning to the west and leading me towards a long dirt road that's teeming with caravans. "Tonight, there will be all manner of Fae in at the palace. There are two portal entrances into the Winter Court. One, the one you entered, is for those we don't know or trust. The other is at the end of this road."

He drops his altitude and I follow, flying just above the tree line. Most Fae are in covered caravans, though some fly along the path above everyone's heads. They don't pay us any mind, and I wonder if that's because they don't see us, or if they don't want to cross Astor. A legion of vampires, or Vampyres as they're called in Faerie, hover behind one particularly large black coach that's pulled by centaurs.

"Night Court," Astor supplies, and then points far in the distance, where giant wolves prowl the path. "That will be Fall Court behind them."

He motions for me to rise and we start flying back. "Where do you put them all?" I ask, battling a particularly harsh updraft.

"Royalty and officials of all courts stay in the palace," he says slowly. "The rest of the citizens stay in one of the further villages. Typically, only the more distinguished Fae attend these affairs. But your mate may be anyone, so for this event, all options must be explored, and all are invited."

I roll my eyes dramatically. The class system seems like bullshit if you ask me.

We return above the clearing, and I pause. "How do I land this thing?" The ground suddenly feels very *very* far away.

"When you have space to come in at an angle, it's best," Astor says. "But for today, go feet first." He positions himself so he's vertical, and his white wings beat at a steady pace as he begins to sink. I snap my eyes shut and trust my wings. Gradually, I feel my body lower to the floor until my feet touch the powdery snow.

Chapter Six

I CELEBRATE MY LANDING by flopping onto my back and making a snow angel. Astor is looking at me like I've lost my damn mind, but I was just *flying*. And I didn't plummet to my death. I already can't wait to get back in the air.

"That was brilliant, Edina!" Two of my fathers appear in the clearing, both smiling proudly as they stand beside Astor.

"Thanks, Five." Yeah, I don't remember any of their names. They're all long and very Fae sounding and the one time I tried to get it right, I mixed up consonants and vowels. Now, I call them numbers.

Five was standing fifth in line when I met the family. He has blonde hair that hangs almost to his waist and is by far the most charming of my fathers. He still doesn't understand sarcasm, but he tries to crack jokes. They're terrible, but I appreciate the effort.

"You should learn our names before the ball," Four chastises, as a particularly large snowflake lands atop his dark skin. He fluffs his silver wings which are so tall they sit higher than his bald head.

"What would be the fun in that?" I tease.

"Well, it wouldn't be fun for you," Astor says. "But it would be most respectful for your fathers."

"Sarcasm, Astor."

"She knows his name," Five grumbles to Four, and I can't help the laugh that escapes my lips. All three men perk up at the sound; Five's light blue eyes even look like they're brimming with tears.

"Is it dance lesson time?" I ask, snapping the men out of whatever moment they were having. Astor nods to us before taking off in the air, leaving me with Four and Five. Four blows out a cold breath, and the snow turns to ice beneath my feet.

"Edina, if you please." He gestures to the ice. I roll my eyes but perform a spell to make it slip-proof. It's something I knew how to do before I came here, but the men made me practice all week since I'll be icing over the dance floor at the ball tonight.

"Today we'll show you a traditional dance," Four says, holding a rigid pose. "It's done to a lighter melody and is fast."

Five sweeps into Four's hold, taking up my position. As he's done in our other lessons, he's playing my part. "Start by stepping back with your left," he instructs.

Music magically fills the clearing, as if the birds are accompanying my training. The men move in steps that remind me of a mix between a waltz and a polka. I'm thankful that Mom—my adoptive mother—made me take dance lessons when I was young, and that Katie made me take ballroom lessons in case I ever needed to be her plus-one to an event.

My fathers whirl around the clearing and I watch Five's feet. When they stop, Five gives Four a flirty smile before they lean in for a quick kiss. I arch an eyebrow as they turn around. They've never shown that level of affection in front of me before.

"Problem?" Four asks, but even he has a rare smile on his face.

"No," I smirk. "I was curious how that all worked. So you're polyamorous?"

"Most of your fathers are only sexually involved with your mother," Five explains. Four tries to shush him, but he waves him off. "Pacome and I are the only ones who are together in that way. We were involved before your mother chose to be with us, and she enjoys when we—"

"I'm good." I hold up a hand. "That's enough of my mother's sex life for today." They both chuckle before Five steps off to the side where he'll call out directions.

"Do you feel comfortable keeping your wings away for the dances?" Four asks. I shake my head. I learned pretty quickly how to retract my wings, but they still pop out at random. "That's fine. Most Fae will wear their wings proudly this evening."

He loops his hand around my waist, beneath my wings, and leads me in the new dance. It takes me a minute to get the intricacies of the steps, but soon I'm able to let Four lead us around the clearing.

"Are you excited for tonight?" he asks. I sigh as I meet his honey-colored eyes.

"Will you be mad if I say no?"

"No." His tone is softer than usual. "Edina, you'll come to find that there is little you can do that will make us angry."

"Challenge accepted," I tease, which is, of course, met with confusion. "Why do you say that?"

Four stops abruptly, motioning for Five to join us. He puts an arm across Five's shoulders, avoiding his long, thin wings, and Five slips his arm around Four's waist.

"You were taken from us," Four continues. "We have prayed to the goddess for your return every second of every day."

"We searched for you too, in the mortal realm," Five adds. "Your mother even sent soldiers, but they returned when we realized the King knew nothing of your whereabouts."

"And now that your back—" Four says.

"I'm not back though," I interrupt. "Not really. Not...yet."

Both men sigh in tandem. "We know, Edina." Five reaches forward and grabs my hand. "But we're happy for any time you have for us."

The weight of his words settles on my chest like a lead balloon. These men don't know me, but they're desperate to. So much so that they scoured realms for me. I can't help but compare them to my adoptive parents, who didn't realize I was gone until Katie told them.

There's no comparison really.

I exhale, releasing a tiny portion of the walls I've erected around my heart. I can let them get to know me. That much I can handle.

"Can we go over the slower dances?" I ask, breaking the heaviness of the moment. "I'm worried I'll step on someone's foot and be murdered viciously."

"No one would dare," Four says sternly.

"Still just joking." Five chuckles good-naturedly, and though I know he has no idea what he's laughing at, it still makes me feel better. I grab Four's hands, and he seamlessly begins dancing.

DAD NUMBER SEVEN, ALSO known as the-one-we're-pretending-isn't-my-biological-father-but-totally-is, sits across from me in a small library in my suite. The white built-in bookshelves run from the ceiling to the plush sapphire blue carpet. There are no windows in this room, but the faerie lights draped across the shelves give the room just enough light without it being too harsh.

Seven is currently droning on about the difference between Magical Creatures in the mortal realm and the Fae that are closest to them in Faerie, but I'm not concentrating. This information is "extra," since I already memorized the royalty coming to the ball tonight. Instead, I'm staring at Seven, studying his brow, which is furrowed in the same way mine is.

"Edina," Seven calls, snapping me out of my daze.

"Sorry. I just..." An unusual emotion surges in my chest, cutting off my excuse.

Seven closes the textbook. "We have about an hour left of your lesson. How about I answer any questions you have?"

"Really?" I already know my question. I've been waiting for an opportunity to bring it up since the tea with my mother. "Can you tell me about hellfire?"

Seven balks. "For your friend's war?"

"It's my war too," I respond. "You told me magic was given to the witches by the Fae. Was hellfire given too?"

"Yes," Seven cringes. "But all Fae who had hellfire have been eradicated."

"How?" I press because this is important. This is the key to winning the war and keeping more people from dying.

Seven's jaw tics, like speaking about it is insanely painful. "Your mother killed them. Her magic...and your magic, we believe, is strong enough to stand against hellfire."

Well shit. "Just ours?"

"We have yet to come across anyone else, Fae or mortal, who can subdue hellfire. And no one is immune to its effects save for those who possess the magic."

I pause, swallowing hard. If what he's saying is true, the fate of the Dark Magic Covens and the fate of all my friends are on my shoulders.

My head spins. I'm not good with pressure, with expectations. I don't respond well to them; I don't like them. I do better in an environment where I can surprise people with how talented I am, not where they are reliant on me to save their lives.

"Don't panic," Seven says softly.

"How am I not supposed to panic?" My voice is shrill and brittle. "How am I supposed to go back there with no hope of a Fae army and tell them I'm the only one who can fight against that magic?"

"You're not without an army."

"Every time I've tried bringing it up since breakfast two days ago, she shuts me down." I stand up, knocking the chair down behind me, and start to pace the small room. "I've been here for six mortal weeks and all I have to offer my best friend is *me*?"

"From what I've heard of your magical training, you are enough." Seven levels me with a serious stare as I halt in my tracks. His sapphire eyes meet my own and I gulp down rising nausea.

"I guess I have to be." I right the chair with my magic and plop down in the seat. Leaning against the table, I press the heels of my hands into my eyes.

"What else would you like to know?" Seven asks. I exhale, resigning to let my insecurities drop until I'm back in the mortal realm.

"Talk to me about tonight," I say. "I'm supposed to look for a mate or whatever?"

"Yes."

"Do you know...what it feels like?"

"Yes," Seven responds again. "It feels like a sharp tug in your gut that leads to everything you didn't know you needed. I know you have shifters in your realm, and they feel the bond when they've had sex, but ours is instantaneous. And when you acknowledge that bond, when both partners accept it, it's..." He smiles softly. "It's magical."

"I'll know as soon as I walk into the ballroom tonight?"

"Only if your mate is present. It's possible they may be from one of the courts that arrive later, or that they're not born yet. That was the case for your mother and me."

"She's your mate?" I ask. "How does that work then? With the others?"

Seven's laugh is low and musical and sounds like the male version of mine. "Your mother was with the others long before I was born," he supplies. "I wasn't thrilled when I found out my mate had six partners she had no intention of giving up, but I was able to get past it. She has an unusual capacity for love that's not often seen amongst the Fae."

"Seriously?"

"You just need to get to know her," he says. "She's the most powerful queen in Faerie and needs to look impenetrable to her constituents and enemies. Sometimes she forgets to remove that mask."

I nod, trying to understand a little better, but I don't. And honestly, if she doesn't help with this war, I'm not sure I care. This whole side quest is a waste of time if I don't come back with an army.

"I have one question for you before your Pixies fetch you to get ready for the ball," Seven says, and I motion for him to go ahead. "We have searched for the man who took you for a long time. Do you know anything, anything at all, about him?"

"He's dead," I say. "My best friend killed him. She didn't know he took me, but that he was wanted for stealing Fae children. I told the queen the other day. I'm surprised she didn't tell you."

His eyes darken, but he nods and stands to leave.

"Wait," I call after him. "Do you think...do you think my adoptive parents knew?" Seven gives me a pitying look that somehow shatters my whole world. Or at least my perception of the world. "Right. Thanks."

His black iridescent wings retract as he exits the library, leaving me alone to get ready.

Chapter Seven

I LOOK LIKE CINDERELLA.

But not in an "oh wow you look like a princess," way. And not in a "tons of tulle ballgown that's somehow modern and adorable," way. In a "there are fucking bustles on my ass," way.

The dress is made of the pale velvet I picked out, but that's about as close to the original drawing as it gets. The top is a sweetheart neckline that gaps over my non-existent boobs. The off-the-shoulder straps that looked adorable and flirty in the drawing are so tight I can't lift my arms above my head.

And the front. Oh goddess, the front. The velvet opens right above my crotch like an open invitation, revealing an underskirt that's white and edged with frilly lace. The back is just low enough to expose my wings but then turns into a twenty-foot train. And I've already mentioned the bustles.

The Pixies piled my hair on top of my head again, this time enchanting snowflakes to sit artfully amongst the curls like hidden sparkles. And they wouldn't even let me wear heels. I'm in these stupid ballet flats that pinch my toes and chafe my ankles.

There's a soft knock on the door to my bedroom before Five peeks his head inside. His long blonde hair is in a sleek ponytail, tied with a navy bow that matches his tuxedo. He looks like he could be a model in the mortal realm. When he sees me, his eyes go wide and his lips flatten into a line as he tries to hold back laughter.

"What did you do to anger Melia?" he asks, amusement coating his words.

"I wouldn't give her my necklace," I say, my plum-painted lips pursing. Yeah, they even managed to pick the wrong shade of lipstick.

"Come," he says, pulling me away from the vanity and turning me around. "Spin," he commands, and I do, shaking my bustles at him as I twirl around. The dress has the added benefit of being super heavy.

"You won't be able to dance in this," he remarks, before snapping his fingers. At his command, both Melia and the Pixies appear with sheepish looks on their faces. "Get the real dress and do her makeup. If she's not ready in ten minutes, Her Majesty will have your heads."

The Pixies squeak and start buzzing around, casting spells to remove my makeup as Melia raises a dark eyebrow at Five. He levels her with a stare fitting of a king, and she snaps her fingers. The dress that appears is still a ballgown, and still poofy as fuck, but it at least it's better.

I conjure an icicle in my hand and use it to slice the gown I'm wearing down the center, staring Melia down the entire time. I swear I see a flicker of respect in her brown eyes as she watches me shed the disaster and stand before her in my white slip.

"You are so much like your mother." Five chuckles from the doorway, heading back into the sitting room to wait.

It takes five minutes to correct my makeup and dress, and another four to walk the labyrinth of hallways to the ballroom. Though ballroom is the understatement of the year. During one of my dance lessons, my fathers took me there so I could get used to the larger space. The room is easily the size of a city block, and even that can't accommodate all of Faerie, which is why Fae with less status come in shifts. They basically have enough time to see if one is my mate and get a glass of Faerie wine before they're ushered out and the next group comes in.

I was also made aware of the royals' schedule. Apparently, today isn't just about me, and they each need their own moment of attention. Their entrances are staggered to coincide with the traditional dances of their courts, which is when I'll be expected to dance with any eligible offspring they have. The Winter Court will be in the ballroom first, so they'll be the only ones who witness my entrance.

Five guides me to two double doors that are manned by two guards in their navy tunics with the silver snowflake insignia. He links his arm through mine and gives it a gentle squeeze. "Ready?"

"Not really." I stare at the doors that lead to the balcony over my mother's dais. I'm not sure why I'm so nervous, but my heart is pounding in my ears and my stomach is in my shoes.

"You'll do great," Five whispers, and nods to the guards, who grip the handles. A second later, the music drifting through the walls comes to a stop.

"It is my great pleasure—" I recognize the booming voice on the other side of the door as Bylur's, "—to introduce Princess Edina of the Winter Court, who has returned to Faerie at last."

There's an uproar of cheers as the doors are flung open. Five guides me forward onto the marble balcony that overlooks the ballroom. Seven waits for us at the stairs, but first I'm to acknowledge the crowd from up here.

"Oh," I breathe, as I take in the cavernous space.

"Princess?" Five asks through his smile.

"It's just..." I swallow a lump. It looks like the party Katie threw me before I emerged, multiplied by ten. Enchanted snow falls from the impossibly high rafters, dissipating before it reaches the guests. Interspersed between the glass windows are white-barked trees that are strung with faerie lights. Ice glitters over every table and every bar, making the whole room sparkle in the soft light. "It's beautiful."

Seven steps up beside me, opposite Five, and the two turn me. We descend the stairs, keeping to the sapphire blue runner. As we walk, I keep my eyes on the crowd, offering a small smile. The room is packed with Fae in more forms than I can register. There's an entire aquarium for water-sprites, who are mermaids completely covered in scales save for their eyes and mouths. Some of the smaller, winged Fae take to the air to get a better look at me.

We finally reach the end of the sweeping staircase and I stop in front of my mother. Five and Seven step back and are quickly joined by the rest of my fathers. Momentarily, they form a line behind me, before sinking to their knees. I don't see it, but I can hear the rest of the ballroom follow suit. When the shuffling has ended, I dip into a curtesy in front of my mother.

I feel her presence more than I hear her move. As instructed, I lift my eyes to meet hers as she casts an intricate spell that weaves a tiara of ice into my curls.

"Edina, you may rise and greet your people," she says in a voice that carries across the cavernous space. I do as she says and turn to find them all kneeling.

"I don't think I've ever brought this many people to their knees before," I mutter.

"Pardon?" my mother asks.

"Nothing." A smile flits across Five's face, and I know he heard me.

With my mother's nod, I hold my hands at my sides and allow my magic to drip from my fingertips. The ice begins to spread, slowly encasing the marble floor in glittering white rime. I follow my magic with the anti-slip spell, so our guests don't slide right out the doorway.

When the entire floor is covered, and the white ice turns crystal clear, the guests erupt in a chorus of applause. They stand and part the center of the room as an army of Pixies roll out a lush blue carpet that leads from the entryway to the throne. It divides the room into two distinct sections, beverages and food and a dance floor.

My mother ascends the steps of her dais and sits back on her ice throne. I follow, standing beside her as my fathers form a line behind us both. Fae crowd along the carpet peering toward the doors which have closed in preparation for the first court's entrance.

"Your Majesty," a guard bellows from the back of the room, effectively silencing any murmurs. "The Royal Family and society of the Autumn Court."

The large wooden doors swing open, and Werewolves in their animal form lead the way, clearing the path for the clump of royalty. I hold my breath, waiting for the pulling sensation Seven described to me, but nothing comes. The doors close again once the last of the procession comes in and I heave a sigh of relief.

Two down, four to go.

I SPEND THE NEXT few hours getting passed from Noble Fae to Noble Fae on the dance floor. Occasionally, my fathers step in and allow me to drink, water only so I remain alert. But even while I take a break, I'm required to meet Fae and engage them in conversation.

Every half hour or so, the general population of the courts is switched out, though I'm never permitted to speak to any of them. Every time anyone enters the room I hold my breath, silently dreading the entrance of my mate.

But if I'm honest with myself, part of me is curious to know what it would feel like to have someone destined for you. Someone who loves you unconditionally on such a deep level that there's no need to keep a distance. No need to run.

After five of the courts have entered, I find myself in the arms of the personal advisor to the King of the Day Court. His skin looks like he spent too much time in a tanning bed, leathery and orange and deeply wrinkled to the point where I can't discern his age. Every time I try to put space between us, he pulls me in closer. It's all I can do to keep a smile on my face as he prattles on about how beautiful I am while the scent of his arousal gags me.

"What do you say, Princess?" he asks. His yellow eyes, which match the straw color of his hair, bore into mine as he licks his lips.

"I—" I have no idea what he asked, but the answer is a hard no.

Someone clears their throat behind the orange male. "May I cut in?" a deep baritone voice asks.

"Yes!" I scream a little too quickly and a little too loudly. I push away from the Day Court Oompa Loompa and hastily bow before jumping into the arms of the other male without even looking at him. To his credit, my savior doesn't wait before waltzing me to another area of the dance floor. As we twirl, I get glimpses of the jilted Fae as he storms over to Father Numero Uno.

"I'm sorry to interrupt what appeared to be a love match," the male dancing with me says.

"No, believe me—" I break off, looking at his face for the first time. His light-brown skin is smooth, and the same color as the long, curved horns atop his head. His hair, coarse black curls, is just long enough to run your fingers through. Full lips are pulled back into a wide smile and amusement dances in eyes that remind me of the Mediterranean Sea.

"That was sarcasm," I breathe, and the Fae arches an eyebrow. "Oh, thank the goddess."

His laugh is deep and raspy yet somehow melodic. "Winter Court Fae are notoriously literal."

"I was really afraid it was everyone." I join in his laughter. "Well, the ability to use sarcasm officially makes you my favorite Fae I've met so far." He smiles wider, revealing dimples that have me transfixed. *Damn, he's fucking cute.* You know, if you can get past the horns. Although having something to grab onto might make things interesting.

I follow his lead around the floor, trying to remember who he is from the countless descriptions Seven drilled in class. He's wearing a deep navy suit that's accented by a teal tie that covers up a peek of black ink on his chest. *Fuck, if he has tattoos, I'm a goner.* My eyes catch on his ears, rounded, but sporting golden jewelry that makes them appear pointed.

"You're thinking too hard, Your Highness," he says, and I roll my eyes good-naturedly.

"I was trying to figure out how to address you," I say as his identity dawns on me. "Is it 'Your Highness' or 'General'?"

He arches a dark eyebrow, and I give him a challenging stare in return. The Queen of the Summer Court is fond of teal, and she has two children, a daughter who is the heir apparent, and a son who is the general of the Seelie Army. They're half-Fae, twins in fact, but the daughter was chosen to rule because she has pointed ears and therefore "looks Fae." You know, because the giant horns spouting from the prince aren't enough to look Fae.

"Since I'm your favorite Fae, you should call me Eldoris," he says smoothly.

"Edina," I respond. His hand shifts on my back and grazes the tiny piece of exposed skin beneath my wings. He's warm, so freaking warm that it feels delicious, and I find myself leaning in closer just to bask in that feeling.

"How have you been enjoying Faerie, Edina?" My name rolls off his tongue in a way that draws my attention to his full lips.

"It's a lot of snow."

"You'll have to journey outside of the Winter Court soon."

"Is that your way of inviting me back to your place?" I tease.

"Diplomatically, of course," he says with a wink.

"Oh, yeah." I bite my lower lip. "That's how I meant it."

The music cuts off, and everyone politely applauds as Eldoris keeps hold of me, his arms solid around my petite frame. His gaze is intense, and his thumb is still brushing my exposed back, heating my blood and making my core clench.

I'm not ready to leave. I like the direction this is headed. But I can't quiet the sound of Three's voice, screaming in my etiquette lessons how I shouldn't linger too long in anyone's presence.

The music starts up again, and I step back. "Thank you for the dance." Eldoris's hand grabs mine at the last second.

"Technically, it was only half a dance," he says, reeling me back into his arms, closer this time than before. "It would be perceived as an insult to my court if we didn't finish."

"Is that so?" He nods, flashing me that dimpled smirk. "So that's a common problem in your court?" I trail my eyes down, only looking up through my lashes after I reach the bulge in his pants. "Failure to finish?"

His chuckle is low and deep as he leans in to whisper in my ear. "Not for my partners."

Yes, please.

I must say it out loud because Eldoris makes a sound somewhere between a hum and a growl. He turns slightly so the tip of his nose *almost* grazes the sensitive spot beneath my ear. It's completely innocent, and yet that small almost contact holds so much promise it sends shivers up my spine. When he pulls back, his pupils are blown, and the heat I'm feeling is mirrored in his eyes. The air between us crackles with an electricity that has every inch of me tightening.

I moisten my lower lip, torn between retreating into friendly banter or taking this further. The ocean and sandalwood scent of him is intoxicating, making me dizzy with lust. Leaving with him would be one hell of a first impression, but there is no doubt in my mind that this male would be worth the trouble I'd get in.

Besides, I'm leaving tomorrow. And I've worked really hard all week. I think I deserve to get thoroughly railed by a random Fae before I go.

"Are you staying in the palace?" I ask as the music swells, signaling the end of the song. He nods. "There's a music room down the hallway, first door on the left if you leave through the main doors. Meet me there after the ball?"

The music ends and he kisses my cheek. "As long as you don't meet your mate."

"I'll see you later." I run my nails down his hard chest before stepping away, and he lets out a low hum of approval.

"Until then."

Chapter Eight

I EXCUSE MYSELF FROM the Fae waiting for a dance and head across the ballroom. Fathers Two and Three are conversing in hushed tones, and I make a beeline for them. Two was one of the fathers who taught me magic. He's built like a freaking house and, even though most Fae are tall, towers over everyone in the room. He runs a hand through his navy-blue hair as Three holds out a glass of crystalline water to me.

I take it and down the whole thing in one gulp, making Three purse his pale lips. Three is my etiquette teacher, and I can tell if we weren't in a crowd, I'd be scolded.

"Refreshing." I hand Three back the glass and his purple eyes widen.

"You were dancing quite close with Eldoris," Two comments, his booming voice even and careful.

"Was I?" I feign innocence. "I was simply swept up in the moment." They won't hear the sarcasm dripping from every word, so I add on a sweet smile to help fool them.

"Spring Court will be arriving soon," Three hisses through his teeth. "Go stand beside your mother." I nod dutifully and prance back over to the dais with a smile on my lips.

"You're in a good mood," my mother comments when I arrive and take my place beside her throne.

"I am." I'm getting laid tonight, and I'm going home tomorrow, with or without my mother's help. Things are looking pretty rosy at the moment.

A throbbing sensation builds in my stomach, and I wince in pain. I take a few deep breaths, fighting the urge to run off the dais and find somewhere to throw up. It happens again, this time more persistent and I double over, inhaling sharply.

"Edina?" my mother asks from beside me, her usual cold exterior fracturing slightly.

"I'm okay—" I manage as the nausea rolls again. It feels like something is behind my belly button and pulling.

"Introducing Her Majesty Queen Titania and the society of Spring Court."

The doors open and I look up, and the entire room falls away as I find a pair of emerald eyes.

My feet move on their own accord as I descend the steps of the dais, drifting down the sapphire runner toward the incoming group. The pulling in my stomach urges me to go faster, but my feet are like lead. His red hair is darker than I remembered, the color almost brown in richness. There's a smattering of freckles across the ridge of his nose that contrast sharply with his pale complexion. His strong jaw is hanging open as he looks at me, and his throat bobs as the tugging around my middle grows persistent.

"Puck," I breathe, and the crooked smile that was charming enough to make me follow him into another realm graces his face.

"Edina," he says. The woman at his side clears her throat, dragging my attention away from the only male who ever made me regret leaving after a one-night stand.

The female is in a green gown as wide as she is tall. Her wings flutter in irritation at my interruption of their ascent to see my mother, her pale features pinched in agitation.

"I suggest you learn your place, girl," she scoffs. "You're in the presence of a queen."

Oh shit. I forgot Puck works for the Spring Court Queen. I dip into a curtsey. "My apologies, Majesty," I say in my clearest voice. "I was just..."

I look up and Puck has broken away from his queen and stands in front of me. He extends a hand to me, and if the noises she makes are anything to go by, Titania is unhappy about this turn of events.

"You're—" I start and he draws me in close, resting his forehead against mine.

"I suspected the night we met," he murmurs. "I wasn't sure since you hadn't emerged. And then you left..."

I've never been one for romantic gestures, for romance of any kind. The whole thing usually turns my stomach. So why is this moment everything? Why is it that the world has narrowed to just the two of us like we're encased in our own special kind of magic? Why is it that all I want is for him to sweep me off my feet and kiss me in front of an entire room of people?

"She's your mate?" Titania screeches, and Puck nods, not turning around, clearly as captured by me as I am by him. His fingers interlock with mine and the pulling in my stomach that made me nauseated moments ago is replaced by warmth and a rush of emotions. Even the scent of the room has changed, filling up with a floral fragrance that invades my senses.

"No." The word is like ice being poured over our bubble, and Puck breaks away from me to turn and look at his queen. The entire guard behind her now has magic shimmering in their hands. Vines spring up between the cracks in the marble and ice.

"Titania, enough," my mother says, and her guards call ice magic to their hands from where they line the aisle.

Titania chuckles and falls into step beside Puck, who now looks between us both confused. "I believe you're mistaken, my dear."

"I'm not." I've never been surer of anything in my life that the male across from me is my mate. Even if I knew nothing about mates, I would have known we were destined for each other.

"But you are." She gives me a cold smile before turning her poisonous glare at Puck. "Puck has been my right hand for centuries. He belongs to me." She leans heavily into the word belongs, and Puck visibly flinches and takes a step back away from me. I chase him a step but am stopped when vines snake around my wrists.

"Titania, enough of this," my mother hisses from her throne. "You cannot deny a mating bond."

"You're right, Gwyn," she says, her smile colder than the ice storm outside. "But Puck can."

There's a collective inhale from all the Fae who have stopped to watch us. "Puck..." I start, but he holds up a hand and I see it. Defeat, resignation, and something cruel in his eyes.

"I'm sorry," he says, his back going completely rigid as he squares his shoulders. "I renounce our mating bond."

It feels like someone just reached into my chest, grabbed my heart, and squeezed until it popped. I gasp for breath as the words ring out in the now-silent ballroom. "No."

"What?" my mother demands, suddenly directly behind me, no longer on her perch on the dais. I can feel my fathers forming a half circle around the two of us, like silent sentinels.

"I renounce the ties that bond us," Puck says. "You are not my mate, Edina of Winter Court."

The queen at his side gives him a proud smile which turns into a sneer when her eyes settle on me. Puck's features twist in pain as the bond between us pulls taut and then shatters into a thousand pieces. It's like someone stabbed me with a hot poker and twisted before dragging it through my entire torso. The pain radiates in every muscle, every bone, every strand of my hair. It hurts to breathe; it hurts when I hold my breath.

My giant dress balloons around me like a gigantic cupcake as I crash to my knees. I clutch my chest as my somehow still-existent heart crashes wildly against my ribcage. Folding in on myself, I bury my face in the mountain of velvet, trying to hide from the thousands of Fae staring silently at this display.

"Get out," my mother says, taking a step towards the Spring Court Queen. My fathers complete the circle that surrounds us, and Five drops to the floor, practically pulling me into his lap. Another one of my fathers holds me from behind, the two hugging tight enough to break me, while a third strokes my hair.

I focus on the only thing I can, controlling the magic that wants to surge from me in a blast of icicles and snow. I hold onto it, willing it to stay within my skin as I shake. Frozen teardrops slide down my cheeks and plunk on the floor.

I hear Titania's cruel laughter as the temperature in the ballroom drops to arctic temperatures.

"Edina," Puck's voice is strained. I don't look up. I can't.

"You have thirty minutes to get to the border or I will slaughter each and every one of you," my mother says, her voice deadly quiet. The sound of footsteps picks up around me, and I dare to lift my head. Between the gaps in my fathers' legs, I see Puck disappearing out the door. He doesn't bother turning around.

The rest of the ballroom is frozen, unable or unwilling to move but not looking away.

"I need to get out of here," I say, standing, and taking Five and Four, who was at my back, up with me. I will not fall apart over a male, and I certainly will not fall apart in front of thousands of Fae. My ice seeps through my veins, strengthening my spine and walling off the crater Puck left in my chest. My mother breaks through the circle to stand before me.

"We'll go back to your room," Seven says, reaching for my arm, but I shake my head and pull away from his grasp.

"No, I need to go home. I need to get out of this realm." Tears are threatening to fall again but I hold them back.

"Edina," Number Five says softly. I turn, my magic rising around me, winter wind pulling sections of my hair from its fancy updo.

"I'm not asking." Ice creeps up my arms.

"You can go," my mother's voice rings out, silencing my magic and the mad thoughts raging in my head. "Astor will accompany you and continue your training, but you may leave."

"And the army?" I ask.

"They will aid your war," my mother replies. "They wouldn't dare deny you that request."

I scoff. Then at least this trip was good for something. Astor steps forward and takes my arm. "Let's go immediately," he says, and his hand squeezes reassuringly. The tenderness has tears threatening to fall again.

"Edina," my mother calls, and I turn back towards her. Her face softens, almost appearing gentle as tears brim in her eyes. "I'm so sorry, my darling. You don't deserve that."

"I'm fine," I say, forcing a smile. "I'm not about to get worked up over a mediocre fuck."

The ghost of a smile crosses her lips, but it's gone before I can register it. "You'll return here as soon as things are settled after the war."

"That's what I promised." She nods, turning on her heel without another word. My fathers disband, revealing the ballroom again. The music starts up, people continue mingling. Everyone avoids looking at me, heads conveniently turned or looking down into wine glasses. Except for one. A pair of ocean-blue eyes find mine through the crowd.

"Astor," I say, turning away from the concerned look on Eldoris's face. My father offers me a small smile, his ice-blue eyes piercing me. "Let's go home."

"Want to try your wings?" he asks, but I don't know that I can summon the strength to fly to the portal. I shake my head, biting down on my trembling lip, and he nods, taking my arm instead.

It'll all be fine once I'm back home. I never wanted forever with someone. I don't need a mate.

I repeat the words over and over as we teleport to the portal. Right before we step into the swirling mist that will take me back to my people, I remove my ice crown, dropping it on the floor and watching it shatter.

Chapter Nine

"I DON'T EVEN KNOW where to start." Katie's voice floats through the open portal door that Vlad had the foresight to send me coordinates to. Astor is behind me, but I lost him as I jogged down the magical walkway a bit. I need to get there before he does, to see my best friend before he's there reminding me of Faerie.

"I have an idea," I say as I jump through the portal door. Katie screams. Her brown hair is loose and wet, and she looks fucking exhausted. Lowell, the wolf, has his arm loosely around her waist but doesn't bother holding her back as she vaults over the table and tackles me. Her momentum sends us backward under the weight of this ridiculous dress.

Katie squeals and scrambles to her feet before pulling me upright so I'm not stuck on my back. "Hang on," I tell her, and icicles appear from my fingertips. I shred the dress, arguably a little viciously, leaving it in ribbons that I step out of. Adriana, Katie's half-sister, sends me a black robe, and I nod my thanks as I use the icicles to cut slits in the back for my wings. I'm not focused enough to keep them retracted right now.

Once I'm situated, we waste no time hugging again, sighing in tandem as we sink into each other's hold.

"You smell different," I say, burying my head in her neck. She usually smells like lavender and vanilla...but there's an undercurrent of rain and something earthy. I've smelled it before, but not on Katie.

It clicks, and my heart drops. That's Lowell's scent, but she's not wearing his scent because they've been close or had sex. His scent *merged* with hers.

Which means they're mates.

My best friend has a mate.

"Is everything okay?" she asks, and I nod, overenthusiastically as I try to mentally calculate things. It's subtle, and I'm not sure if that's because she's human or if they haven't solidified their mating bond, but I'm certain Lowell is her mate. And judging by the way he's staring at her, he's in love. He won't reject her. He'll be happy when he finds out they're mated.

I'm so happy for her. No one deserves unconditional love more than my best friend.

But I can't breathe.

"Yeah," I gasp. "I just...I needed to get out of there. But the Fae agreed to help. I'm not sure when they'll send reinforcements since they have no sense of urgency but they're coming."

"What did you have to promise?" Vlad asks, and I notice him for the first time as Katie leads me to a chair beside her.

"It's not important," I say, brushing her off. I need to get out of my head. I need to not think about any of this.

"E—"

Astor stumbles through the portal doorway and his eyes find mine instantly. His look is one of pure pity, and it makes me want to throw things.

I put on a good mask, one that makes me just look tired. I introduce Astor, make a joke about not being well-received in Faerie for my sarcasm, and listen as Katie and her friends catch me up on everything that's happened in the mortal realm since I left. The most troubling of which is that Katie's father went rogue, killed the king, and almost killed Lowell.

They make plans, and I zone out, trying to keep myself from falling apart. I can't let Katie see how badly I'm hurting. I know her, and she'll drop everything to comfort me, which I love about her. But I also know she needs a minute with Lowell. The only thing that breaks my trance is a moment of tension between Vlad and Adriana. But even that doesn't last.

They come to whatever conclusions they make, and everyone stands to leave except me and Vlad. I need to talk to Katie; I need to tell her she's mated in case she doesn't know.

"Katie, can I have a word?" Vlad asks, and I lounge back in my swivel chair. Katie ushers Lowell back to their room, and Vlad fixes me with a glare that says *get the fuck out.*

"E—" he says, exhausted.

"I need to talk to my best friend," I tell him, the sternness in my voice covering the fact that I'm breaking. "And I bet our conversations overlap so I'm not going anywhere."

Vlad rolls his eyes but looks away. "The golden magic–"

"Was were-magic, right?" Katie asks, and Vlad's eyebrows shoot up to his hairline. "It was the same color as Lowell's eyes."

"It usually manifests after.... everything is solidified." I don't know why he's not saying they're mates, but they clearly haven't solidified their bond. He continues prattling on about her connection to Finley and her mate.

"Does Lowell know you're mates?" I cut in, and Vlad rolls his eyes. I give him a sickly-sweet smile that makes him smirk. He really should know better. Obviously, they taught me about mates during my trip to Faerie. "Just another one of the many perks of being Fae...scenting mates." I mime gagging.

"Did you know before you left?" she asks.

"No, babes," I promise. "I got better at understanding my powers in Faerie. When did you find out?"

"Earlier tonight. Lowell doesn't know yet."

"You should tell him," I say, my eyes misting against my will. "If I can scent it on you, the other Magical Creatures probably can too."

"Plus, she screamed *he's my fucking mate* in front of Lowell's entire pack," Vlad adds.

"I'll tell him, just not tonight," Katie says, and I narrow my eyes. "I just... is it so bad that I want the moment to be special?"

"No," I whisper, squeezing her hand. "That's not bad."

"I'll tell him tomorrow," she says, and I give her a reassuring smile as she stands. My breaths are coming in faster, and my magic is right at the surface of my skin.

"Oh, E?" Katie stops in the doorframe, turning over her shoulder. "When we got the news that the king died...we were at a werewolf orgy."

"Oh fuck all the way off," I scream as she cackles and runs out of the room. Vlad joins in her laughter. And this moment, me being pissed at my friend for attending a werewolf orgy without me, makes me feel one iota normal again.

I HEAD DOWN THE hall towards my room in the coven, my shoes and dress discarded in the war room. I shift the black robe all the coven members wear so it stops falling off my shoulders.

A strong hand wraps around my elbow, tugging me sharply down another hallway at warp speed. "Vlad," I protest, as I register his blonde hair and imposing frame.

He doesn't stop until we reach a simple room, the black comforter thrown off the bed. As soon as the door closes, he pushes me against it and slides his tongue into my mouth.

"Vlad," I say sharply, pushing him back. He goes easily, but his eyes are swimming with emotion. You'd have to be blind not to see that something is going on between him and Adriana, and she clearly slept with Rodger. I have no interest in being in the center of some weird love triangle.

"Please, E," he whispers. He looks as broken as I feel.

"I won't be the other woman." I lay my palm on his chest. "So, if you're with her and just having a fight—"

"We're not together," he swears and leans in, kissing the corner of my mouth.

"How not together?"

He sighs heavily. "I fed from her when I shouldn't have." I arch an eyebrow. "I'm not going to explain why it's a bad idea to feed from someone you're attracted to. It's long and boring and full of vampire politics that you won't care about."

"Fair."

"But she offered, and I was weak. One second I'm feeding on her and she's humping my leg—"

"There's an image I could have lived without."

"—the next, we were naked and about to fuck."

I blink. "I don't understand the problem."

"I lost time, Edina. Completely blacked out. I don't know if it was bloodlust or..." Vlad swipes a hand down his face. "Do you know how dangerous that could have been? I could have killed her. Or worse." There's pure terror in Vlad's eyes. In the short time I've known him, he's always seemed strong, unshakable. Not right now. Right now he looks haunted.

"I backed off," he continues. "Told her we couldn't be together that way. And she fell into bed with the next man she saw." He steps in closer and threads his fingers through my hair. "So we're very much not together."

I find myself nodding. Vlad was there for me when I needed him. It would be really shitty of me to abandon him when he's in need. Plus if I'm ever going to get to sleep tonight, I'll either need to be drunk out of my mind or fucked into oblivion.

"It's just about the release," I assert. "A distraction." Vlad nods, not even trying to smile. I shuck off my robe as he starts on his suit. We undress in a flurry of movements before colliding back together in a bruising kiss. He walks me towards the bed, flopping onto the mattress and pulling me with him so I'm straddling his hips.

"Lube?" I ask. He points to the nightstand, and I summon the bottle, squirting some into my hand and coating his cock.

I toss it beside us when I'm done and slowly sink down until he's completely sheathed inside me. "Fuck," I breathe. When I'm adjusted to his size, I start to move, and my body gets the hint to lean into the pleasure.

Vlad's fingers dig into my hips as I grind on his length in slow, teasing circles, working until I find the spot that feels best. His hand slides to my clit, working my sensitive nub in short, fast strokes.

My breathing increases as my pleasure approaches that precipice. I pinch my nipples as Vlad matches my thrusts, bucking me against him and making me cry out. I'm right there. So close I can taste it.

I look down into emerald eyes and a face spotted with freckles. My breath catches.

"Shit," I mutter, slowing my motion until I'm completely stopped, unable to move off Vlad but unable to start up again. I'm trembling with the force of keeping my emotions locked down. I squeeze my eyes shut, willing the image of Puck away from my mind.

Even though I haven't used my safe word, Vlad remains frozen, his hands resting on the mattress beside my legs but not touching me. "E—"

"I'm fine," I get out. "Just...fuck me from behind." I climb off him and lean over the mattress with my ass in the air. He turns on his side, facing me and I inhale through my nose, willing my tears to stay away.

"We don't have to," Vlad says softly, brushing a piece of hair behind my ear. "We can talk about it..."

"Please," I echo his earlier statement. "Please, Vlad. I don't want to talk. I just want to forget."

Vlad sighs and gets off the bed. He tenderly kisses my shoulder, before threading his fingers into my still-constructed updo and yanking me up. He slams into me and we both groan at the sensation. He does it again, and again. Faster and faster. Until I can't think of anything. Until the whole world is narrowed to the feeling of Vlad fucking me.

"Just like that," I gasp as he leans forward, hitting the perfect spot inside me. His hands move from my hair and my hips to the sides of my throat.

"This okay?" he asks, and I scream out my answer a moment before his large hands cut off my air. I let the oblivion wash over me as spots dance in front of my eyes. He releases me just enough so I can get a breath, and I scream as the orgasm that's eluded me takes over my body.

I tremble beneath Vlad, barely able to stay on my feet as he resumes his furious pace until he groans his release. We both pant, gasping for air as our bodies cool down. Vlad slowly extracts himself and disappears, only to return with a washcloth to clean me up. I stay exactly where I am, my face buried in the sheets because I'm crying, and I really don't want to be the girl that cries after sex. My body doesn't get the memo.

Vlad dumps the cloth before pulling me into his arms, guiding my head to his chest as I continue to sob against him. He doesn't mention it. Doesn't ask what's wrong again. He just holds me and draws soothing lines up my spine, between my wings.

When my tears have dried and my breathing has returned to normal, I look up at the vampire. His mouth is set in a thin line, his jaw working like he's also trying not to lose it.

"We can talk about it if you want," I offer. He kisses the top of my head and I sink back into his hold until I feel his breath even out in sleep before I slip out of bed and return to my room.

I CAN'T SLEEP. I think I get an hour or so, but that's it. After I can't stare at the ceiling anymore, I get up and start wandering the halls of the coven. I'm surprised to see so many people awake after the battle yesterday, but over half the coven is up and walking around. But I don't know anyone here. I left before I got the chance to meet any of the Dark Witches, and now everyone is looking at me funny. Some are clearly frightened of me, while some look at me like I'm their savior. Katie must have told them I was securing an army.

I end up in the mess hall, sitting at one of the cafeteria-style tables with a cup of coffee that Katie would wrinkle her nose at since it's more sugar than coffee. I'm absently stirring the mocha syrup that's settled at the bottom when Astor finds me. He offers me a tight smile as he walks past and gets food. I stare into my cup, avoiding his gaze as he approaches and sits. He puts a croissant in front of me.

"You need to eat," he says. I don't bother arguing. The flaky pastry turns to ash in my mouth. "Would you like to train today?" he asks, sipping his cup of tea.

"Sure." We fall into silence until I finish the croissant.

"I've never dealt with this," he whispers into his cup.

"A rejected mating bond?"

"Comforting a daughter." The dam of my tears breaks again, and I don't fight Astor as he wraps an arm low around my waist. I bury my head in his shoulder.

"It hurts," I tell him. "Not just emotionally. It's physical. Like every bone in my body is being broken repeatedly. Like someone yanked my stomach out of my throat."

"I'm sorry," Astor says. "I wish I could help with the pain."

The honesty is refreshing. He doesn't tell me it'll get better or that I'll move on. He just acknowledges my pain and is there for me. It helps. Not enough to take away the feeling, but enough that I can think. I can't imagine anything ever taking away this feeling completely.

"Astor, I need to call my adoptive parents." He cocks his head to the side. "I need to know if they knew." The thought has been niggling at me since I emerged, and I need answers.

He nods solemnly. "Would you like me to be with you while you complete the call?"

I mean to say *no* but find myself nodding *yes*.

Together, we walk through the tunnels to the hills outside. The weather is still cold, but compared to the Winter Court, it's balmy. The sun is blocked by the layer of gray clouds that crowd the hills, mirroring my mood, and the air is thick with the promise of rain.

I walk a little way past the entrance and sit on a patch of grass. Astor sits beside me as I take my phone from the pocket of my jeans and dial my mom's cell.

"Edina?" Her New York accent comes through the receiver. "We were so worried."

"Hi, Mom."

"Where have you been, cupcake?" my dad asks. "Katie called and said you weren't going back to school. Then there was all this business with the King and Katie's father, and we were worried--"

"I was in Faerie." The silence on the other side of the phone is deafening. "I guess that answers my question."

"Edina—" I can hear the hysteria building in her voice.

"You have to understand," my dad starts. "Before we got you, our daughter died during childbirth."

"And I sustained enough damage that we couldn't have children," my mom adds.

"Magical adoptions are hard," Dad continues. "But we found a man saying he could help us for the right price. We'd pay anything to have a child. All he told us was that you had magic and your birthdate and time."

"We didn't find out you were Fae until just before your fifth birthday."

"Around the time you sent me to boarding school," I say, and my mother gives a broken sob. "Were you distancing yourself because of the legal ramifications or because you were afraid of me?"

"We wanted you to have the best magical training you could before—"

"Before I emerged," I finish. "Which was the most terrifying and painful experience of my life. You didn't think to let me know? To give me some kind of warning?"

"We didn't know how to tell you—"

"You had sixteen years to figure it out." It feels like I'm breaking all over again. My life is just one series of rejections after another.

"Do you know my birth parents looked for me?" I ask. "For twenty-one years, I had a family who loved me enough to search through another realm for me. And you just shipped me off to a boarding school and pretended I didn't exist."

"We love you," my mom sobs. "We didn't know what to do. We were scared and didn't want to lose you."

My lower lip trembles, but I clamp it down and go numb.

"Katie and I are working with the Dark Witches to help restore the imbalance of the Kingdom." My voice is robotic, devoid of all warmth and emotion. "I suggest you stay out of Europe, but to be safe, avoid all the highly populated magical areas."

"Edina—" they start.

"After the war, I'll be returning to Faerie to live with my real mother and fathers."

"Edina!"

"Thank you for..." I clear my throat. "Thank you for sending me to school with Katie, I guess. She's really the only family I've known anyway."

"EDINA!"

"Goodbye, Allison. Jack." I hang up the phone and call water to my hands. It surrounds the phone until the screen sputters and goes out. Then I harden the water to ice, exerting enough force that the phone bursts into shards.

I hug my knees to my chest. I didn't think I could feel any more broken than I did an hour ago. *I was wrong.*

I'm aware that I'm staring blankly ahead at one patch of grass as tears fall down my cheeks. I'm aware that Astor places a hand on my elbow and stays with me. I'm aware that as the sun dips beneath the hills, rain starts, but I don't get wet, which means Astor has shielded us. But it feels like I'm *watching* everything happen to me instead of *experiencing* it.

Maybe my body just needs to be numb for a little while. Maybe the reprieve from the pain is a good thing.

Probably not.

"Edina." Vlad's voice snaps me out of my trance, and I turn to find him standing in the mouth of the coven. "You need to come. Katie lost her fucking mind and thinks she's going to the palace alone. She won't listen to the rest of us."

I release a breath, wipe away the residual tears, and stand, steeling my spine. I break free of Astor's shield, aware he's on my heels but not turning back. "Let's go." I reach Vlad, and he puts a hand on the small of my back as we head to the war room.

AUTHOR'S NOTE

Thank you so much for reading this novella about Edina and the start of her journey (you read that right)! Her full-length novel, Of Ice and Heartbreak will be available in December of 2023!

Reviews are SO important to Indie Authors, and I'd greatly appreciate it if you could take a few minutes to leave a review on Goodreads and Amazon

Need to chat about this little slice of pain? Join our Readers' Group or follow me on TikTok.

All links can be found on my website: www.marianneascott.com

About the Author

Marianne A. Scott has been writing since she was a kid. When she was always singing, those stories appeared in song form, when she majored in acting, they appeared as screenplays, but novels and short stories were what she returned to when inspiration struck. Each and every story was driven by characters and love, and, most of the time, the hope that there was something fantastical about this world that us humans just haven't discovered yet.

When not writing, you can find her with her Kindle and a latte, sitting opposite her husband in their New Jersey home. In her other life, she teaches tiny humans how to sing, passing along her love of musical theater to the next generation.

Also by Marianne A. Scott
The Made from Magic Series

Made from Magic

Made to Conquer

Made to Rule

A Court Where I'm Freezing My A** Off (a Made from Magic
Novella)

The Fae Romance Series
Of Ice and Heartbreak (December 2023—Preorder Now)

Acknowledgments

First and foremost, I'd like to thank all of you who have made it this far. Thank you for helping me realize this dream.

To the best husband in the entire universe of the world, thank you for always supporting me, and for always comforting me when the imposter syndrome hits. Thank you for being a sounding board when I need to talk through plot points, even when I don't listen and just need to talk at you. And thank you for taking care of all the behind-the-scenes things I wasn't prepared for when I went into self-publishing.

To my amazing parents, thank you for being excited every time I tell you page read numbers and Amazon rankings. You're my biggest cheerleaders and I thank you so much for your never-ending support. And for John, thank you for reading and providing me with up-to-date texts to let me know what you think. PS: I hope you all collectively skipped some sections.

To my writing partner/sounding board/plot-hole cannon Rachel, thanks for listening when I talk about this series every single week during our chats. Thank you for every note, every hour spent listening to me dissect the magic system only to scream "there's a spell for that" when I couldn't answer the question you asked, and every creativity check-in.

And last but not least, thank you to my family and friends who are literally the most supportive people in the entire universe, including the amazing readers in the GrossBooks Readers Group! I am so lucky to have you all!

www.ingramcontent.com/pod-product-compliance
Lightning Source LLC
Chambersburg PA
CBHW072035170626
46811CB00008B/3083